GENE ISLE

BY CRAIG BALCOMB
ILLUSTRATED BY LOVE QUETEE

Gene Isle
Copyright © 2022 by Craig Balcomb

All rights reserved. No part of this publication may be reproduced, distributed, or transmitted in any form or by any means, including photocopying, recording, or other electronic or mechanical methods, without the prior written permission of the author, except in the case of brief quotations embodied in critical reviews and certain other non-commercial uses permitted by copyright law.

ISBN
978-1-952182-80-8 (Paperback) $11.99
978-1-952182-81-5 (eBook) $2.99

TABLE OF CONTENTS

CHAPTER 1	THE BEGINNING	1
CHAPTER 2	IN TROUBLE	15
CHAPTER 3	MOVING INLAND	19
CHAPTER 4	A NEW FRIEND	27
CHAPTER 5	THE LAB	39
CHAPTER 6	THE DOCTOR FLEES	57
CHAPTER 7	THE ATTACK	61
CHAPTER 8	THE RESCUE	67
CHAPTER 9	DEBRIEFING	75
CHAPTER 10	THE RETURN	85
CHAPTER 11	BACK TO THE ISLAND	93
CHAPTER 12	THE DOCTOR SAILS	107
CHAPTER 13	CALEB RUNS	109
CHAPTER 14	NEW GUINEA	113
CHAPTER 15	BACK TO BASE	115
CHAPTER 16	JAKARTA	119
CHAPTER 17	AT BASE	125
CHAPTER 18	CHINA	129
CHAPTER 19	ON THE RUN	133
CHAPTER 20	GOING HOME	135
CHAPTER 21	CALEB RUNNING	141
CHAPTER 22	EPILOGUES	145

CHAPTER 1
THE BEGINNING

The car bounced and shook. It vibrated roughly as it passed over every crack and pothole in the road. The affect was churning Naledi's stomach. Her meager breakfast was threatening to return up on her. Sitting back in her seat she tried to calm herself. She tried to relax and keep her stomach in check. That was not easy as the taxi sped rapidly over the rough pathways of the port. Warehouses zipped past the windows as Naledi looked for any sign of her destination. It could not be much further she thought. She hoped it wasn't, she wanted out of the taxi as soon as possible. This was not how she wanted to be spending her morning. After several minutes of rapidly navigating the back roads and alleyways of the port the cab came to a quick stop. Naledi leaned forward and reached into her hip pocket. She pulled out her wallet reached inside it and grabbed out her money. The taxicab had come to a stop and had parked in front of a long wooden pier. Naledi took a moment to steady herself. She then reached over the backseat and paid the cabbie. Slinging a backpack over her shoulder Naledi jumped out of the cab and began to jog down the pier.

With her feet pounding over the wooden planking. Naledi hurried down the pier. She didn't want to be late. It was bad enough she had been woken up so early by the telephone. After answering the phone, she learned she had to report immediately to this port for a field assignment. Naledi could not understand why she was needed. She was not a field agent, she worked in a forensics lab. She had been told almost nothing about the assignment except to report here as quickly as possible. As a result, she had been in a non-stop rush all morning. Now, she jogged as quickly as she could. Her eyes scanned over the boats as she ran. She tried to find the one she was supposed to go to. After more than halfway down the pier she thought she had spotted it. There at the end of the pier was what looked like a large luxury yacht. As she got closer it was clear that it was much more than a luxury yacht, it looked more like a research vessel. There were multiple antennas and electronic equipment attached to the top of the ship. Naledi came to a stop in front of the boarding ramp. She paused to catch her breath. "You're late!" shouted a voice high above her. The voice came from the bridge of the ship high above her. Naledi looked up while still breathing heavily. As she looked up, she saw a tall man in his mid-thirties with broad shoulders, scraggly unkempt auburn hair, a scraggly beard, and a grim expression on his face. "Stop stalling and get aboard." cried the man leering down at her. Adjusting her backpack Naledi stood up and dashed several yards up to the boarding plank. From there she ran quickly up the ramp. A few moments later she stepped onto the deck of the ship. "Hurry up! I haven't got all day! "Shouted the stern man at the bridge high above her. Naledi walked stepped up onto the ship. The strange man snarled down at her. Naledi wandered toward the rear railing.

Her backpack slid off her shoulder. Naledi let the heavy load drop onto the deck. Looking around there was no one else to be seen. She walked up to the rear railing. Naledi was a tall dark young African American woman as she leaned over the railing.Naledi wondered why she was here. She was not a field agent, and she was rather new. She began to feel the deck vibrate under. She heard someone shout" Castoff!" Several men scurried about the ship untying ropes and tossing them away from the ship. The roar of engines grew louder, as they started up. She leaned over the bow's railing looking out over the water and saw the water churn as the propellers whipped the water into a heavy white froth. She could feel the deck vibrate under her feet as the ship's engines rumbled to life. Her stomach still churned queasily. It had not fully settled after the taxi ride. Naledi looked out across the water hoping to spot a dolphin or something else interesting, but the ocean was almost as still and smooth as glass. The only waves were created by the ship's propellers as they churned the water and pushed the ship forward and away from the dock. "Hey there," came a voice from behind her. Naledi turned. She saw a man that was trotting up toward her, waving at her. A stocky young man with curly sandy-blonde hair wearing jeans and a khaki t-shirt came jogging up to her. "You must be the science tech they sent for." He said as he came to a stop in front of Naledi. "Yes, I was called early this morning and told to report here. I have a master's degree in biochemistry. I got my degree two years ago just before I was hired five months ago and then stationed out here in Hawaii. They called me in a couple hours ago." She replied. The young man stuck out his hand, "Great, I'm Greg. And you are?" "Naledi" she replied as he shook her hand. "Naledi, I have never heard that name before. Where are you from?" Greg pronounced her name slowly as if he were trying to decipher it." Where are you from?" asked Greg. She replied "I was born in a small village just outside Maseru, Lesotho in Southern Africa, but I grew up in Ohio. After stumbling over her name Greg just grinned at her. "You are not exactly what I was expecting." He said. "Oh, and what were you expecting." Greg cringed, "Never mind. It's not important."Naledi said nothing and just stared at Greg. She could guess what he had expected. He probably expected some pudgy middle-age white professor from an ivy-league school, not a tall young woman with Basotho parents. Naledi never liked it, but she reluctantly was getting used to the reaction people had to her. They reacted her based on her physical appearance most people did not believe she was remotely capable of what she had achieved academically or in her career. She was just a woman, and a black woman at that. She guessed he was not expecting or comfortable with her being a woman, especially black woman. Naledi asked "Why was I assigned to this mission?" Greg answered, "For your science background." "That does not make sense. There are people in my department with far more experience than me. So, why me? Was it for an appearance of diversity that I was chosen?" "You said you were hired five months ago. LIFO, that is your answer." Greg continued. "LIFO! What the hell is that?" Naledi asked. He answered "It is originally an accounting term meaning Last In-First Out. You were hired very recently so you have almost no seniority. As the last hired you were the first to be assigned to a mission like this." He waved his hand at her and called out "Follow me. Let me show you where to park your stuff." Greg said as he led Naledi across the deck. Naledi picked up her belongings and followed him. She followed him to a bulkhead door. Inside the door was a set of metal steps leading down into the hull of the ship. She followed him down the steps as she reached the bottom of the stairs, she could see a series of cots lining both sides of the hull. A group of young athletic men in their early to mid-twenties sat quietly on their cots. They all stared at her wide-eyed as if in shock. Naledi felt extremely uncomfortable, she felt a strong mood of disapproval from these men. Greg introduced Naledi to the team of field agents after they reached the bottom the stairs. All the men were very muscular with grim dominant expressions across their faces. Beginning from the left Greg said "This is Sam." Sam had short black hair in a crew cut. He sat on his cot sharpening a knife with a whetstone. Greg continued introducing her to the men around the room he introduced Naledi to Fred, Fred was vainly combing his long auburn hair. Max came next. Max sat reading a copy of "Soldier of Fortune" magazine. Naledi thought he looked like a mercenary. He had several issues of the magazine scattered across his bed. He scowled up at Naledi. Max looked like a man who wanted to be an action hero, like in the movies. Michael was next. He was a muscular young blonde man, who looked like a competitive weightlifter. He had prominent square chin and he was working out with heavy hand weights. He displayed his biceps proudly. Bill followed Michael; he was a handsome young curly redhead. Finally, there was Hank. He sat on his cot busily cleaning and assembling an assault rifle. Naledi felt very out of place amid this testosterone fueled pack of young men. Except for the handsome Bill, all the men looked like potential mercenaries to Naledi. Greg led Naledi to the empty cot between Bill and Hank. She set her backpack down on the cot. She sat on her cot next to her backpack. She pulled out a pair of binoculars from her backpack. Looking around her, she saw that Greg had already left. She was sitting alone between these young testosterone fueled field agents. She could feel their eyes upon her, but their stares were more disapproving than sexual. She could feel them judging her professionally. It was clear to her they resented having a woman on the mission, especially a woman of her heritage. Since their eyes never looked at her above her shoulders. She was sure they were judging her more than just professionally Naledi turned and climbed up the steps. She wandered across the deck to the rear railing. Standing at the stern of the ship she looked out over the ocean, it was more interesting than looking out at the Great Lakes. She could see that she was now several miles away from the harbor on the open ocean waters of the Pacific. Looking out across the ocean the only thing that could be seen were small white caps stirred up by the breeze. There was no sign of land or other ships nearby, nothing to suggest a possible destination. Even with her binoculars she could see no sign of land or another ship. With her right hand resting on the railing, she walked around the ship. She looked out across the water hoping to spot something of interest. As she scanned the still ocean waters, she heard a voice shout "Hey you there come with me. Are you the science tech they sent for?"*A strange man tall man in his mid-thirties with crew cut hair that was slightly gray at his temples looked into her eyes. Greg said, "Sir this Naledi, she is the Sci tech that was sent to us." Greg turned to Naledi and said "This is Frank Fetters. He is in command of this mission." Frank ordered "Come and follow both of you. We have things to do." Naledi followed Frank and Greg across the deck and then up a stairway of metal steps and into the bridge of the ship.* They all gathered around a control screen. Frank pointed to an elderly white-haired man at the wheel of the ship. "This Is Captain Putnam; he is piloting the ship for me." The three of them all gathered around a tabletop screen. On the screen appeared to be some form of a radar display. In the upper right corner, there was a blinking dot. Pointing at the dot Frank said, "This is our destination." "A blinking dot?" Naledi asked. Frank answered "That dot is more than just a blinking dot. It represents the ship of the smugglers we are following. They have robbed several colleges, universities, Research and medical facilities of advanced scientific equipment. My mission is to find out who is stealing the equipment and why." Looking at Naledi he continued "Our mission is to arrest them, secure and return the stolen equipment." He said then stared at Naledi. "Your job is to determine how they are using the equipment and for What they are trying to use it for. There is a large amount of stolen equipment on that ship. Where are they taking it to who and why?" Naledi stared at the blinking dot wondering what it meant for her. She stared at the video screen. "I see no signs of land. So where are we going?" she asked. Frank impatiently replied, "We are going after their ship. We managed to secretly place a homing device on it. We follow them. Their destination is our destination. Do you understand Now?!" "Yes Sir."Naledi meekly replied Since it was clear the meeting was at an end. Naledi turned and slowly exited the bridge. Greg followed a few paces behind her. She eased her way down the stairs then she strolled across the deck. She returned to the ship's railing. She leaned over the railing. Her fingers clutched the railing for security as she strained her eyes gazing at the distant horizon. She searched the horizon intently to her great frustration there was nothing visible on the ocean waters between her and setting sun. There was not the slightest hint of land or another ship. Naledi stared out across the ocean waters. As her eyes scanned the ocean, she began to wonder how long it had been since they left the harbor this morning. It had been an awfully long day. Seeing nothing along the horizon Naledi Let go of the railing. She turned around and walked back across the deck. She then walked down the stairs into the hull of the ship. At the bottom of the stairs, she searched for her bunk. She squeezed her way through the crowd of young men all around her. When she finally navigated her way to her bunk she sat down. She laid down ignoring everyone around her and their unwelcoming reactions to her. She did her best to ignore the insults around her about her heritage and being a woman. It was not easy to ignore the foul comments swirling all around her. She closed her eyes and tried to sleep. She tossed and turned as thoughts of this day and the days ahead swam through her mind. Sleep did not come easily for her as so many thoughts raced through her head. She wondered if what Greg said was true. Was she here because she was the newest hire in her department. Maybe there was some truth in it, but she was certain there was a bit of racism involved too. Being assigned here got her, the only black woman, out of the department. Maybe they were hoping she would not return. She knew a few co-workers and her supervisor would not be upset if she did not return. Eventually, she did fall asleep even despite all the snoring around her. When she woke up before dawn, she walked up the stairs to the main deck. In her left hand she carried her binoculars just in case they might be useful. As she stepped on the deck Naledi could see the orange glow of the morning sunrise throughout the sky above her. She enjoyed the beauty of the morning sunrise against the ocean horizon. She turned and looked out ahead of her. She was surprised to see a beach and palm trees arching out over a beach and leaning toward the bow of the ship. Naledi watched the beach and jungle slide passed her eyes as the ship cruised slowly along the island's shoreline. There was a lot of noise and commotion behind her. The men below scurried out of their bunks up the metal staircase and out onto the deck.

Frank lumbered down the stairs from his commanding perch up on the bridge. As he stepped onto the deck he walked over beside Greg. Soon all the men huddled around Frank and Greg. Frank started telling them all about his plan of action. Standing alone off to the side Naledi strained to hear what was being said. Frank began his lecture to his men "Men, the enemy has sailed their ship to the other side of this island. That is why we are cruising along the Western shoreline. So, they do not know we are here and to find a good place to drop anchor, we will land on shore and search the island. We will begin a reconnaissance patrol after sunset at 19:00 hours. Get yourselves and your equipment ready. We have no idea what we might encounter." The men dispersed to gather and check their supplies and weapons. Naledi looked over at Frank quietly asking "What about me? What do I do?" "You and the old captain stay here. I will call you when you are needed, not before then. Stay on the ship." She felt dejected she came all this way and now she felt they did not need or want her. She wondered why she had been called if they did not need her. Naledi wandered up to the bridge. There she found the old man, Jeff Putnam, at the wheel. "I guess it is just us staying behind," She lamented. Mr. Putnam looked at her, "That is fine by me." He replied. "I have no desire to go trudging through thick tropical vegetation after sunset. There is no telling what they will find or what will find them in that jungle." He replied. Naledi watched Mr. Putnam carefully guide the ship along the coast. She watched the island beach glide by. She stared up into the trees and thick tropical vegetation. She could hear the calls and songs of a wide variety of birds. She could hear them, but she had difficulty seeing any birds among the trees, because the foliage was so extremely thick. In fact, the only birds she could clearly see were the seagulls that flew along the beach as well as over and around the ship. Feeling unneeded She went below and secluded herself on her bunk. While the men plotted their course of action. Naledi rested on her bunk reading a recent genetics journal and munching on mini chocolates. She heard the big splash of something falling into the water. The crew had just dropped the anchor of the ship. A moment later the ship came to a halt. Naledi felt a sudden jerk as the ship came to an abrupt stop. She left her bunk and walked up the stairs onto the deck. She looked around and saw the men gathering around Frank. Frank discussed his plan with his team. He then organized the men into a marching order. He placed the youngest agents, Bill, and Hank up at the front. These two men were to take the point of the mission. Frank spent several minutes telling his point men exactly what he expected of them. Naledi watched and listened as best she could, but she could hear only a little bit of what was said. Frank and his troops lowered themselves into a rowboat down to the water below. It took just a few minutes of them all rowing before they landed on the beach. Frank leapt out of the boat as it neared shore and scurried through the low tide water up onto the beach. He turned and shouted at the men to follow him. Within a few minutes Frank and his men were huddled together up the beach a few yards short of the tropical forest. Frank repeated the marching order and his plan of action to the men. After Frank repeated his instructions, the men begin their journey across the island. As the sun began to set the team set out to find the criminals they had been pursuing. Bill and Hank lead the team into the jungle first followed by the rest of the team. Immediately they turned on their flashlights the fading sun light and thick foliage made it difficult to see. Even with their lights on it was a challenge to see through the foliage. As Frank followed his men into the jungle. They disappeared. Naledi leaned over the ship's railing and strained her eyes. She could not see the team. Bill and Hank led the team through the foliage attempting to create a path leading to the opposite side of the island. They began slashing at vines, shrubs, and tall weeds to try to cut a path through the thick jungle. As hard as they cut their bayonets made very little progress cutting through the jungle vegetation. The jungle slowly got darker as the minutes passed, and the sun was setting. The few rays of sunlight that illuminated the jungle faded slowly away. Now they could only see by the limited glow of their flashlights. After over an hour of hiking through the jungle they were less than a quarter mile away from the ship. They still had a long way to go before reaching the other side of the island.

Hank looked ahead of him. He was hoping to find an easier pathway. Unfortunately, the light from all the flashlights only created a lot of shadows and no good illumination. Scanning the terrain in front of him Hank thought he spotted a possible alternate path. Hank noticed off to his right there appeared to be a stream. The stream was snaking its way between the trees. Hank decided to investigate it more closely. He waved over at Bill. Signaling Bill to follow him. Hank slowly and carefully walked down the embankment and into the stream. Bill entered the stream just a few yards ahead of Hank. The water seeped in and filled his boots. Bill could feel the water slosh around inside his boots as he began to walk forward in the stream. The stream began to turn a corner around to the right several yards ahead. Hank lost sight of Bill as he turned the corner out of sight. As he reached the corner Hank felt a strong tug on his backpack. Seconds later he was pulled backward and lifted off his feet. Hank's body was swung forcefully through the air. Before he could understand what was happening his head slammed against the trunk of a thick palm tree with a loud "thwack!" Hank's body went limp and was dropped into the stream. The rest of the team began firing their weapons.

Naledi gripped the railing as she stared into the darkness. She knew she could not see them, but still she continued to stare in the direction that the team had left. Well after sunset more than a half hour after the team entered the jungle, she heard the loud popping sound of sporadic gunfire. She glared into the darkness. She began to wonder what was happening. "Are they in trouble? Have they run into the enemy already?" no answers were visible. Naledi began to worry as the gunfire faded and then stopped. She climbed the ladder back up to the bridge. She went over to Captain Putnam. Maybe he had heard something from Frank over the radio. Unfortunately, he hadn't." I am Sorry Frank insisted on radio silence. There have been no messages since they left." Naledi and Captain Putnam looked through the window toward the beach. They saw nothing at first. Several minutes later a group of figures moved out of the jungle the silhouetted figures moved forward onto the beach in the direction of the boat. "Is that them?" Naledi asked. "I don't think so" replied the captain. He reached for a revolver hidden under the control panel. He stepped toward the window and looked out toward the beach. As he stood at the window there was a large popping sound. The window shattered. Naledi saw the captain fall back and land on the floor. Blood flowed from a large red spot on his neck. Seeing his body fall to the floor Naledi collapsed to the floor too. She looked away from him and began to crawl across the floor to the opposite side of the bridge. She crawled to the doorway on the opposite side of the bridge. She looked back over her shoulder Captain Putnam was not moving. He was obviously dead or dying. Naledi crawled out the doorway onto the walkway surrounding the bridge. She peaked around the bridge briefly back at the beach. The silhouetted figures were moving closer to the ship. She could faintly hear voices. They did not sound familiar or friendly. She hoped she had not been seen. Who were these people she thought? Where was her team? In a hurry and not wanting to take chances She slid down the railing of the stairs to the main deck below. As she crawled along the deck, she heard footsteps moving up the metal ramp. She hoped they had not seen her. Naledi pulled herself under the railing. She hesitated for a second, she pushed off away from the ship and dropped into the water. The weight of her shoes and wet clothes pulled her down deeper in the water. That was not so bad since she did not want to surface, and risk being seen. The weight of her clothes did make swimming more difficult. She held her breath and tried to pull herself through the water as far and as fast as she could. She swam as best she could just below the surface. After swimming several yards her lungs began to beg for air. She ignored the feeling moving further along in the shallow water. Finally, she risked breaking the surface. With her mouth at the surface Naledi took a deep breath and then dove back below the water. She swam as hard as she could. She had no idea how far she had swum, but she wanted to put as much distance as possible between her and the ship. She held her breath as best she could while pumping her arms hard to pull herself through the water. Every couple of minutes her head would surface just enough to take a deep breath and then submerge back under water. Slowly the water was getting shallower as she put more distance between her and the ship. As she continued to swim her left hand scraped against some sharp rocks in the shallow water. She cut the palm of her hand on the rocks. The pain of the cut was magnified by the saltiness of the water Her palm bled. She hoped the blood would not attract any predators, but she had not time to worry about that. Naledi swam away from the rocks into slightly deeper water. The weight of her soaked shoes made it difficult to get any propulsion from her legs, instead they dragged her legs down. As a result, her knees began to touch the bottom After about fifteen minutes she was becoming exhausted. It was getting ever more difficult to pull herself through the water. She felt her knees brush the sandy bottom of the bottom of the shallow water. Feeling the soft sand under her legs she reached down with he hands to feel the soft sand below her. On hands and knees, she began to crawl through the sand out of the tide up to the beach. As she crawled, she tried to keep sand out of the recent cut on her palm. She made her way slowly up the beach. As she crawled in-land she occasionally looked over her shoulder back the way she came. She could see the silhouette of unknown figures moving about the boat. One of the figurines looked very large and not human. She heard a loud splash as Captain Putnam's body was tossed overboard. She hoped they did not know about her. She crawled up the beach into the shrubs and vegetation behind a large thick palm tree. She sat down, rested, and breathed deeply. After the long hard swim and holding her breath, she was enjoying the feel of each deep rejuvenating breath of air. Breathing felt wonderful at the moment. She leaned her back against the tree and closed her eyes. She was exhausted. She was not trained for physical action. Her work was primarily done in the lab or in an office. She did not choose her career for survival training or to become an action hero. She was a forensics lab technician not a soldier. From behind the tree, she glanced back at the boat. The silhouetted figures were gone, but there was an orange-red glow emanating from the boat. It took Naledi almost a minute staring at the boat to realize it was on fire. As she watched the glow of the flame grow brighter. The tendrils of flame reached ever higher as the fire became an inferno quickly engulfing the ship. Naledi sat behind the palm tree gently brushing sand from the palm of her hand. She carefully tried to sweep the sand out of the cut on her hand. She was concerned about the possibility of infection. She tried to wash out her wound with the ocean water, the salty water stung her hand as she washed out the wound. Unfortunately, she knew there was no way to thoroughly clean and sterilize the wound under her current circumstances. As huge flames turned the ship into burnt cinders Naledi lay back in the thick vegetation, closed her eyes and tried to rest. Sleep quickly overcame her. She woke up suddenly. She sat up straight and shaded her eyes from the late-morning sun. She was scared. She had only meant to rest her eyes, not sleep through the night; she could not sleep. She looked back towards the ship. It was gone. After burning what was left of it sank below the water. Naledi saw no one. She looked left, right and every direction possible. She sighed in relief. There was no sign of any pursuers. Although she saw no one pursuing her, she did not want to take any chances. She tried to stay hidden. Besides, she did not know what happened to Greg, Frank, and the rest of the team. She began to move away from the beach to the interior of the island. She did not know what her location was or which way she should go. For now, she stayed as low as she could and slowly moved inward. She walked at a crouch through the dense vegetation. She paused trying to decide which direction to go. She turned left and continued moving. Having chosen a direction to pursue She turned. She assumed she was heading north, but she was uncertain. All she was sure of was that she was moving further toward the center of the island. She faced a thicket of vines and bushes ahead of her. Looking at the dense vegetation in front of her she became aware that she had no tools to cut through the jungle under growth. Despite this disadvantage, Naledi began pushing her way into the jungle. She kept moving deeper inland. The weeds cut and scratched at her legs and arms. The tiny cuts and lacerations itched. She was well-rested, but hungry. The shrubs and vegetation around her offered some tempting fruits and wild vegetables for a hungry woman. No matter how hungry she was she dared not give into temptation. She had no means to determine if the fruits and vegetables were toxic or not. Although her stomach growled at her she could not take the risk. Her stomach was grumbling at her. She ignored it and pushed her way further into the jungle vegetation. She hoped Frank and the other men were out there somewhere If they were there was slim chance that she could meet up with them. Unfortunately, she had no idea where they were in the jungle or if she was headed in their direction. She moaned in pain as she moved slowly through the weeds and bushes. The scratches on her body caused her skin to itch and bleed slightly. Naledi hoped no one was looking for her on the path she was making. She would not be difficult to find. As she moved forward through rough vegetation ants and other bugs bit at her skin. Mosquitoes feasted on the scratches and open wounds on her legs and body. The tropical insects feasted on her as she crawled slowly through the rough and thorny vegetation. The tropical heat and humidity caused Naledi to sweat a great deal. She could feel sweat rolling down her forehead. Her sweat was also pooling on her chest. Her shirt was soaking wet and sticking to her skin like flypaper. She was at a risk of dehydration. If she did not find water soon, she was risking heat stroke. Naledi looked around for any clue to water. She wiped the sweat from her brow and continued moving forward through the rough vegetation. She was so hot she wanted to pull off her shirt, which stuck uncomfortably to her body. She did not dare pull her shirt off it provided her a small amount of protection from the rough abrasive vines, bushes, and ravenous insects in the jungle that she was moving through. Sweat dripped from her body. Her shirt was as wet as a washrag. She could hear the birds and small animals in the trees. She heard movement in the bushes up ahead of her.

She looked around scanning the area in front of her to determine the source of the noise. She strained her eyes attempting to see what was ahead of her. There clearly was something 20 to 30 yards ahead of her. She hoped it was a member of the crew. To Naledi the creature in front of her appeared to be some type of small mammal that was mostly hidden behind the bushes. The more that Naledi studied the creature the more she speculated as to what it might be. After studying it for several minutes it was apparent to her that the creature was some form of small island herbivore. It resembled a small deer like animal. She watched and studied the animal. The small deer moved a little further inland to Naledi's left. It then bent down low. Naledi began crawling toward the deer as quietly as possible through the thick jungle. When she got less than a dozen yards from the creature the small deer thrust it' s head up. It looked left and right. Seconds later it leaped up and sprinted out of sight back into the jungle. As the animal disappeared into the jungle Naledi began to follow its tracks. She crawled following the tracks she noticed that the edges of the hoof prints were damp almost muddy. It gave Naledi a sliver of hope. She moved faster while ignoring the scrapes and scratches against her exposed skin. After a few more yards she reached the end of the deer's tracks. She looked up and could not believe her luck. Before her eyes was a freshwater stream which flowed through the island toward the sea. Naledi bent over the stream. She dipped her face in the cool water and drank deeply. She drank greedily replenishing her dehydrated body. Once she filled her belly with fresh water, she stopped drinking. She rolled over and rolled her body into the stream. The flowing water cooled, soaked, and rejuvenated her severely over heated body. Naledi laid in the stream as long as she dared. She wanted to enjoy the feel of this miraculous oasis as long as possible. She did not know when she would get this lucky again. After almost an hour laying in the water she crawled out of the stream. She crawled up between two thick bushes. There she rolled over on her back and fell asleep. Her physical exhaustion kept her asleep through the night.

CHAPTER 2
IN TROUBLE

Frank awoke with a severe pain in his head. As he became more fully awake, he could feel pain throughout his body. His ribs felt as if someone had used them for boxing practice. Slowly he opened his eyes and looked around the room. He tried to determine where he was. Clearly, he was not in the jungle anymore. The room he saw looked like a clinically clean sterile room with white walls. It felt like he was in a hospital or operating room. He looked around for his men. He only saw Greg laying on a table about 30 feet on the other side of the room. Greg appeared to be unconscious. Greg looked like had had more hair on his body than before. Frank looked over Greg. He noticed that he was strapped down to the table he was laying on. There was also an IV tube running down to and attached to his left forearm. Frank wondered why Greg had an IV attached to him. Frank tried to move. He quickly noticed his wrists and ankles were strapped to the table he was lying on. Frank could not move no matter how much he tried. Frank noticed that Greg had a nasty looking wound across his forehead "Where were the rest of the men?" He wondered if his men were alive or held prisoner elsewhere. He was depressed over his failure as a leader and being placed in this strange situation. Frank thought that other than Greg he had not seen any of his team. He wondered where they were and what had happened to them. Frank struggled to remember what happened after he and his team had entered the jungle. He remembered leaving the ship and guiding his team off the beach. He could not recall anything happening after they were about a quarter mile into the jungle. It had been difficult to see through the thick canopy of leaves and vines blocking out the quickly setting sunlight. When they were deep in the jungle Frank remembered hearing, Hank cry out then two gunshots. He remembered Bill and Hank were on point leading his men into the jungle.

Somehow, they had been attacked and then Frank and the whole team were ambushed. A moment later Frank felt something hit him in the head then slam his head against a tree trunk. After that he blacked out. All of that occurred last night. Frank looked across the room at Greg. He tried to guess his condition as Greg laid on his back strapped down to a table. Frank heard a latch click. He saw a door open that he had not noticed before open. Through the door stepped a short man with scruffy gray hair and slightly hunched shoulders. The man shuffled across the room and then stood next to Greg. Frank watched the strange man stand over Greg studying him carefully. "What are you doing to him?" Frank shouted. "Making him better." Replied the strange white-haired man. "How? Frank asked What's wrong with him?" Frank asked. "I am tending to his wounds and caring for him medically" answered the small man. "What's wrong with him?" Frank repeated. "Your friend has a severe concussion and a few cracked ribs." Came his answer. "Where are the rest of my men?" Frank questioned the strange man. "I do not know about anyone else. You were brought in with a mild concussion and a few cuts. That is all I can tell you." After answering him the man walked over to Frank. "Enough questions. I have important work to do." As the strange man made this statement Frank felt a sharp pain in his left arm. The man injected him with a strong sedative. In less than a minute Frank was losing consciousness again. His mind faded to black. The small old man sat on a stool next to Greg and began attending to him. He inspected the Intravenous lines feeding a slow drip of chemicals into Greg's veins. While the strange man hovered intently over Greg's body, Naledi began waking up beside the stream on the other side of the island.

CHAPTER 3
MOVING INLAND

Naledi woke up and looked around. She tried to think of how to proceed moving further into the interior of the island. Moving forward into the island was her only option to hopefully find a way off the island and to safety Naledi did not see any sign of people following her, but she could not be sure. She was safe for now, but someone might still be pursuing her. She decided that the best way to move further inland would be to follow the stream. She reasoned that by walking in the stream she would make fewer if any tracks for anyone to follow her.

Naledi got to her feet and walked over to the stream. She slowly stepped into the water her feet were quickly soaked as water filled her shoes. Although it was uncomfortable to have water sloshing around in her shoes. There were definite advantages to walking in the stream the most obvious was that she was not leaving a trail behind her, also by walking in the stream she did not have to cut her way through her way through the dense vegetation the path in front of her was easier to navigate. The disadvantage was that her feet were soaked as she walked and that her feet and ankles were exposed and vulnerable to anything living inside the stream. Naledi began walking further and further up the stream and into the jungle. She hoped to find her former shipmates, but she had no idea where they were. She kept moving slowly inward as she walked up the stream. Occasionally she sat down on the bank of the stream and took a brief rest. As she rested, she drank some water, splashed some water over her face and arms. She also looked around her in the vain hope of finding anything edible. As Naledi walked further through the stream. She was slowly finding it more difficult. Walking further into the island, the bottom of the stream became muddy. As the stream bottom became muddier her shoes began to stick to the bottom in the mud. The muddy bottom stuck to her shoes making each step more difficult. By the middle of the day. Naledi was getting tired the effort of walking through the muddy bottom and the heat of the day was becoming intense. A couple of hours past midday Naledi stepped out of the stream and sat down beside a tree. She leaned her back against the tree to rest. To her shock and horror, she noticed small leeches sticking to her ankles and lower legs. She had not thought about this possibility and now she struggled to think how she would remove them by hand. She had no tools or chemicals to help her remove the leeches. She wanted to relax in the shade of the tree out of the intense heat of the heat of the midday sun. Unfortunately, she would now have to spend her time carefully and painstakingly removing the disgusting leeches. So, she began carefully working at removing the leeches by hand. It felt disgusting as she used her fingernails to pry the blood engorged leeches off her skin. It took her well over an hour to completely remove all the leeches she had acquired. Naledi pressed small vine leaves over the open wounds left by the leeches. She was concerned that the open wounds would leave her exposed to infection and invite more insects to harass and feast on her unprotected body. Now that she had removed the parasites from her skin. Naledi considered carefully what to do next. She knew she had to continue her journey into the island, but she did not want to risk more leeches by walking through the stream again. After careful consideration, she decided that the best thing for her to do was to walk along the banks of the stream and not in the stream itself. So, she got to her feet and continued walking along the banks of the stream. By doing this she knew that she avoided the risk of more leeches, but she also lost the advantage of not leaving any visible tracks behind. She didn't like losing this advantage that she gained by walking in the stream, but she was willing to risk it to avoid the risk of further leeches. Naledi tried to console herself with the thought that she had walked long enough in the stream that anyone following her would've lost her trail. She knew there was still a chance that someone who would find her tracks and follow her, but it was a risk she had to take. She walked alongside the stream further and further into the interior of the island. She hoped that she might get lucky and find the men who had left the ship on patrol to pursue the thieves that they were after on this mission. Unfortunately, she had no idea where they were or what might have happened to them. She only hoped she might encounter them and that they might have food and provisions for her. She grudgingly walked along the bank of the stream. It is not what she wanted to do but it's what she knew she had to do. With each step she took another step closer to the center of the island. As she walked, she thought about all that happened to her in the past few days. She slowly went over in her mind everything that happened since she boarded the boat and took this adventurous cruise to the island that was probably off the charts. She thought about the death of Capt. Putnam and the burning of the ship. So much had happened in the last few days. Now she had to concentrate on what she needed to do to survive. She needed to find food and the members of the patrol that left the ship. She scanned and looked all around her to see if there was anything, she knew was edible. Unfortunately, so much of the vegetation was unfamiliar to her and eating anything that she was not certain of was a risk. As she plodded along the side the stream, she noticed one of the trees had small red bananas hanging from the it. They were not like the big yellow bananas she used to buy the at the grocery store. They were not the large yellow bananas she normally found in the produce aisle. They were more like the exotic small red bananas which She found in the foreign food produce section. She had never eaten bananas like these, but she figured the risk in eating these was rather low. So, she picked up a few small red bananas that had fallen to the ground. She sat down and began to eat them. Her stomach was growling she had had almost nothing to eat in over a day. Her stomach and her body were running on empty. Only fear and adrenaline had kept her going, but now her energy level was so low she could not continue on adrenaline alone for much longer. She sat at the base of a large palm tree. One by one, she slowly ate several of the small red bananas. She was surprised how good they tasted but that might have been because she was starvingly hungry. In a matter of minutes, there was a small pile of banana skins stacked up beside her. After eating about five or six of the bananas. She was beginning to feel full. She started to feel sufficiently rejuvenated by the intake of food. Naledi stood up, ready to continue her journey. She picked up a few small bananas and carried them with her. Despite being a tropical island. Naledi had not seen any coconuts, or citrus fruit on any of the trees. She was uncertain when she would find food again. She considered it a small miracle that she found these bananas. So, as a precaution, she decided to take some with her. Now with her stomach full for the first time in more than a day. She began to continue her journey. As she continued walking along the bank of the stream. She looked around her to see if she could find any other sources of food. As she looked about her, she also kept alert for any signs or tracks of the men that left the ship, the previous night. She hoped to link up with the men from the ship for safety, for rations and other provisions. She also hoped they might have some knowledge of the island and what had happened since they left the ship. While she constantly turned her head, looking around her, she could see no indications of the team that left the ship or of additional safe food sources. She felt very alone scared and frustrated. With each step, it was becoming clear to her that she was totally on her own. She would have to rely on herself. There was no one else to assist her. Capt. Putnam was dead, and all the other men were missing. Naledi continued to move forward. She tried not to think about what might have happened to the rest of the crew. She also tried to keep from thinking about what fate awaited her up ahead. She put one foot in front of the other and kept walking down the bank of the stream. It was the only thing she could do was to keep moving, everything else was out of her control. Sweat rolled down her for- head and puddled up on her chest. As the heat of the day intensified her body became covered in sweat. To relieve herself of the heat and discomfort of the sweat. She occasionally splashed water on her face and arms. Naledi enjoyed warm weather, but the intense heat and humidity of this Tropic environment was becoming too much for her. She started to walk a little bit faster. Looking up ahead, it appeared to her as if the tropical foliage were becoming thinner. Maybe she was reaching the end of the jungle she thought to herself. More light was making its way through the trees, branches, and vines. She could see more clearly now in the jungle than at any time since she entered it. After another hour Naledi was pushing her way out of the tropical jungle and onto rocky ground. She was now clearly far from where she had started the night before. She was far from where the journey began. She began to walk across a flat rocky surface. Unfortunately for her the rocky terrain provided no shade. That made the rocky surface hot on her feet with each step. She could feel the heat of the rocks through her shoes on the soles of her feet. The sun had baked the rocks heating them up. Now she could feel that heat on the bottom of her feet as she walked. She walked faster and a bit more lightly due to the heat of the sun baked the rocks. Naledi was concerned that the heat on her feet could cause blisters. Without shade from the trees, the intensity of the sun was beating down on her forehead and her skin. She began sweating heavily. It was necessary for her to drink more water from the stream and occasionally splashed it across her face and arms. It was a struggle, but she did her best to keep cool and hydrated. That was not easy with heat beating down on her from above and from beneath her feet. Naledi noticed as she walked the ground was slowly rising. There was a slight upward angle to the rocky surface. She was She was making a steady climb along the upward grade of the rock face. The stream ran along a narrow cut in the rock. To Naledi's eyes, it was apparent that the water running down the rock face had eroded a pathway through the rock. She continued her slow climb upward. With each step the angle, up was getting steeper making the climb more difficult and tiring. Naledi wondered at what elevation she was. She wondered how far up from her starting point at the Sandy Beach had she risen? She had no way to measure the distance. She did not know she where she had begun. She knew her breathing had become a little bit more labored. As she had climbed higher the air started to get thinner. She was at a higher altitude than when she started. Naledi's legs were getting sore as she pushed harder to climb up the steep incline, her body ached all over, especially in her legs and back. This adventure was not fun for her but, it was necessary, if she were to survive. She had not received survival training. It was not necessary. She normally worked in a lab processing DNA evidence. It was becoming late in the afternoon. Within a few hours, it would be sunset. Naledi looked around. Naledi looked around trying to decide where might be a good place for her to bed down for the night. The terrain was so flat and barren. It was hard to find any place that would be safe to camp for the night. Although she had seen no signs that she was being followed. She could not take a risk. She wondered; did anyone see her jump off the ship? If they didn't, she might be lucky. If they did, chances are good that someone was looking for her. Could she really be that lucky? She had no idea who the strangers were that shot the captain and burned the ship were or what they wanted. If they saw her. She was sure they would be searching for her. Naledi continued walking up the rocky slope. All the time she was wondering who the strangers were and what her fate was to be.

Caleb was certain there must have been someone else aboard the ship it was obvious to him after searching the living quarters of the ship. There had obviously been more bunks and possessions there than the number of men he encountered and defeated. Clearly, there was at least one person that was unaccounted for. Based on the belongings on the beds. It must have been a woman. How had she escaped; he did not know. Caleb was certain he had taken every precaution to ensure that no one got away from him. Now, he was searching the island to find the woman that had eluded his grasp. He could not let anyone escape him. He found a few tracks in his search. The woman was obviously clever, resourceful, and alone. He hoped to find her as he the climbed the rock face. He had to catch her. He could not let anyone interfere with the work being done on the island. Caleb was a thorough individual he would not let anyone get in his way, no matter how unexpected it was. The person he was chasing now was very unanticipated. He knew the federal agents were chasing him, but now he had eliminated them. All except this one unknown person that was completely unexpected. Now he was on course to eliminate this last witness in his path. Caleb was frustrated. It was much more difficult to track his quarry on the hard rock surface. He had not had much difficulty tracking his prey through the jungle. In the jungle. There were several indicators, some of them subtle, on the path his prey had taken. It was not that difficult for him to follow the path through the jungle. The rock surface now created a greater challenge. Despite this difficulty, he persevered and walked slowly up the Rocky surface. Caleb took the lead in marching up the rock surface. His mercenary team followed behind him. He was certain if he followed the same course he was on when he left the jungle that he would eventually catch up to his quarry. He was followed closely behind by his team.

Naledi woke up as the morning began. She stood up and stretched her body felt stiff and sore from sleeping on such a hard surface. She felt rather refreshed from a good night's sleep, despite having traveled non-stop through the jungle and across the island. She began her journey a new as the sun rose in the sky. She looked around trying to determine which way she should go. Moving forward, she noticed a slow, steady decline across the Rocky surface. It soon became clear to her that she was now moving downhill. Standing at a higher point of the island. She looked out to try and see what was ahead of her. She could see a short way across the island. At the base of the rocky hill. All she could see were the treetops of a forest terrain. Cautiously she moved down the hill trying to be careful not to slip and tumble down the rock face. As she reached the bottom of the hill, she began to reenter the tropical forest. As she entered the forest. She looked about trying to find the stream again. It took her almost half the morning of searching, but she finally found her way back to the stream. Upon reaching the stream she leaned over and drank deeply from the stream. She had to rehydrate herself before continuing. She got to her feet stepped into the stream and began walking further into the island. As she walked through the shallow water of the stream.

CHAPTER 4
A NEW FRIEND

She thought she saw some movement up ahead of her. The movement she saw was brief and fleeting she could not make it out clearly, but it was there. What could it be? She thought to herself. She looked more carefully to see what it was. After about a minute, she noticed it again. She concentrated hard to try and make it make out what it was. In the trees up ahead of her, she saw a tall furry figure moving between the trees. The figure stood up right, it was close to 6 feet tall. Naledi tried to think what it could be. Was this a new threat she had to worry about? It couldn't possibly be a bear she thought would not be here in the tropics that seemed very unlikely. She continued walking moving further toward the center of the island. Again, she saw the strange figure. As she got closer the figure appeared to have a posture and stature of a person, but if that were so who could it be? She studied the figure cautiously, as she stepped closer to it. As she got within a few yards of the figure. It confused her. It had the shape of a man, but everything else about it seemed so animalistic. What or who was this creature? Naledi was baffled. She could not figure out what stood before her. She was also a little scared of it. It stood at least a head or more taller than herself, at 5' 8". It was definitely stronger than her. It was broad in the shoulders and very muscular. Its body and face were covered with a thick layer of coarse brown fur.

Caleb followed by his cohorts reached the summit of the rocky hill. He noticed an alcove between the large boulders. Searching this natural alcove. Caleb noticed the vague remains of a campsite. He was convinced the woman he was pursuing had slept here recently. Caleb was delighted he was still on the trail of his quarry. He had not lost the track as he feared he might on the rocky surface. He was confident he would be able to eliminate her soon. He believed he was within striking distance of her. His hunt would be over soon.

Naledi slowly edged her way into the forest and closer to the creature. She looked nervously up at this strange creature. She was uncertain what to make of this creature. It did not seem to be anything that belonged on a tropical island. Nervously she took slow steps closer to the creature. She looked quizzically upon it. Strangely enough as she stared at the creature, she noticed it staring back at her. It seemed as curious about her as she was about it. The two of them stood staring at each other for several moments. Although they stood just a few feet apart, neither one took any action toward the other. Naledi cautiously extended an open hand toward the creature. The creature stared at her slow movement. Her fingertips were close to brushing against the creature's thick, shaggy fur. The creature hesitated. It stared in disbelief. A moment later it extended its long arm out toward Naledi. Tentatively they both reached out toward each other. With her hand trembling Naledi reached out. A moment later their fingertips touched. The creature touched her extended hand and recoiled as if an electric shock suddenly ran up its arm. At this Naledi withdrew her arm. The two stared at each other, both not sure what to do next. The creature looking down at Naledi made a guttural groaning sound. She could not understand what the creature was doing. Was it trying to communicate she wondered. Naledi looked up at the creature and it looked back down at her. "What do I call you?" She asked. A puzzled look came across the creature's face. The creature made another guttural sound. "Should I call you Urrrgh? She asked in an attempt to verbalize the sound he was making.

The creature vigorously shook his head from side to side. "No? Then what do I call you?" She asked. The creature knelt to the dirt beneath his feet. Naledi watched in fascination. The creature. Slowly drew one fingertip across the dirt. Naledi watched his movements wondering what he was attempting to do. In the dirt he drew the letters "ALDO. "Aldo is that your name?" She asked. The creature nodded his head in agreement. Naledi looked up at the creature and said kindly. "So, your name is Aldo. "Hello Aldo. I am Naledi it is a pleasure to meet you." Naledi smiled up at Aldo. She extended her hand offering to shake his. As Naledi became more familiar with Aldo and tried to learn more about him. Her pursuers continued following her trail. Caleb searched the ground in front of them for any sign of his quarry. As he and his team slowly edged down the slope. As he headed out of the Rocky terrain and into the forest evidence of Naledi's trail became clearer. Caleb was certain now that he would catch up with her soon. Slowly he followed the tracks and moved continually closer toward Naledi.

Naledi was busy attempting to communicate with Aldo. Her attempts seemed only partially successful. Based on his reactions Naledi believed that he was understanding what she was saying. Unfortunately, she could not understand him. No matter how hard Aldo tried all he could do was make growling and guttural sounds. He could not speak clearly enough to be understood. Naledi smiled up at him encouragingly. She tried not to show her frustration at their one-way communication. She did her best to explain to Aldo slowly and clearly everything that had happened to her in the last few days. Aldo stopped trying to speak. He looked up at Naledi quizzically. He then got down on his knees in with his fingertip in the dirt. He spelled out the words "why you here?". Naledi looked

down at what he wrote. She began as best she could to explain why she had arrived on the island. Aldo listened carefully as Naledi explained her journey and the assault on her boat. Aldo looked up and past Naledi. He growled and stared up beyond where she was standing. This startled Naledi until she heard a shout from behind her, calling "there she is, get her!". Caleb and his team were not far behind her and closing quickly. Naledi saw three men approaching. They were moving quickly down the slope toward her and Aldo. The man at the rear of the group was shouting instructions. Naledi felt a need to run, but she froze where she stood. Aldo stepped in front of her and picked up some large stones as the men came closer. "Get her," shouted Caleb. The men ran forward toward Naledi as they attempted to grab Naledi. Aldo stood in their way. The first man swung his arm at Naledi, but Aldo grabbed his arm, giving it a strong twist. The man cried out in pain. Naledi could hear bones cracking. The man fell to his knees clutching at his arm while writhing in pain. Another man quickly tried to grab her until he felt Aldo's fist slamming into his face. The force of the blow made him crumble and fall to the ground. Caleb pulled his pistol out of his holster. Aldo threw a large stone before Caleb could take aim. The rock slammed against Caleb's temple. It shocked and stunned him, causing him to drop his pistol. Aldo ran up to Caleb. He picked up the pistol and threw it behind him. Naledi saw the pistol fall several yards in front of her. Aldo punched Caleb and then subdued him, holding him to the ground. Caleb looked behind him and shouted, "Kill Them!!!" Several yards behind everyone appeared a strange angry looking beast. Naledi stared at the hostile looking beast. She raised the pistol she just picked up. She held it tightly in both hands. For a brief moment she thought this new beast looked like Aldo. As it got closer it looked more like an old movie Werewolf on steroids. It was getting closer to Aldo and preparing to attack. Naledi pointed the gun at it. She aimed and pulled the trigger. The new beast staggered, but it did not stop as it charged at Aldo. Naledi shot three more times the werewolf-like beast collapsed to the ground. It bled profusely from its wounds.

Naledi was thrilled, happy and proud as the beast lay on the ground bleeding. She thought that these men must be the same ones who attacked the ship last night. They must have shot Captain Putnam dead. Naledi walked slowly up to Aldo. She wondered why Aldo defended her so fiercely. She looked up at him with concern and gave him a thankful hug. Aldo put his hands on Naledi's shoulders holding her close to him. She was now indebted to Aldo, the strange man creature. As Aldo held her close to his body Naledi could feel his soft, thick fur on her face. The soft cushion of his fur felt oddly soothing to her. She felt comforted by the embrace of this man-beast. Naledi wondered how Aldo could tolerate surviving in heavy fur in the oppressive humid tropical heat. She gazed up at Aldo and he released her embrace of him. Caleb groaned and attempted to get up. Aldo kicked him hard on the side of his head. He collapsed into unconsciousness. Naledi turned she stepped passed Aldo and began walking toward the center of the island. Aldo quickly stepped in front of Naledi he held out his hand as if to signal "Halt!" He stared down at her shaking his head "No." She looked up at him and explained to Aldo "I have to go. I need to find the men that sailed with me here. I don't know where they are or what happened to them. I need their help to escape this island." Aldo stared down at her. He turned and began walking inland. He waved his arm for Naledi to follow him. She began to walk behind Aldo in his shadow. She followed him. Naledi was glad to have Aldo's help and his company. She felt less alone and worried as she walked behind him. Naledi wondered why Aldo was helping her, but she was glad he was acting like her guardian and guide. Together they walked further inland. Periodically they sat under a tree to rest or drink from the stream and cool off. Late in the afternoon as they rested under a palm tree Naledi leaned against Aldo's body. She rested her head on his furry belly and closed her eyes for a few minutes. As she rested Naledi felt her head and hair being gently stroked. It felt like she was being petted. Was this huge man-creature becoming affectionate to her? She opened her eyes and stood up. Naledi looked into Aldo's eyes. He looked at her. There was a long silence as Aldo slowly got up on his feet. They resumed their journey together.

The sun was setting. Daylight was fading. Aldo led Naledi to a shady spot between several trees. He looked over at her while patting his hand on the ground. "You want us to camp here tonight?" she asked. He nodded his head "Yes" and sat on the ground. Slowly and carefully Naledi sat down beside him. As Naledi sat down Aldo turned and walked off. Naledi settled herself under a tree wondering where Aldo went and why. The shadows grew longer as the sun was setting. Naledi sat on the ground thinking she had thought Aldo was her friend, but in his absence, she wondered how much she could truly trust him. After about five minutes that seemed like an eternity of doubt to Naledi Aldo slowly returned." What had he done while he was gone?" she thought to herself.

Aldo walked casually back toward Naledi with his hands extended out in front of him. Naledi could see bananas, berries and other fruits and berries cupped in his outstretched hands. Obviously, he had been foraging for food for them both. She accepted the food he handed to her. She began eating the berries she had ignored before fearing they might be toxic. She thought they must be safe if Aldo handed them to her. The berries tasted sweet and succulent in her mouth. It reminded her of eating wild blackberries as a child. She enjoyed the fresh berries and bananas. As she ate Aldo laid down to rest. Naledi leaned against his body as they both quietly ate their dinner. After finishing her meal and feeling a bit full. She laid her head down against his soft furry belly. She closed her eyes and curled up beside Aldo. She was so exhausted she was asleep within minutes. Eventually Aldo fell asleep too. He was also very tired. Through the night they slept close together with Naledi resting her head on his belly like it was a pillow.

As the morning rose so did Aldo. He carefully lifted Naledi's head from against his body and gently rested her head on the soft foliage beneath him. As he set her down and let her sleep he wandered off into the tropical forest. The morning sunlight began to seep through Naledi's closed eyelids. Soon she could no longer ignore the dawn. She opened eyes, stretched, yawned, and looked around for Aldo. She turned this way and that looking all around for him. He was nowhere nearby to be seen. She wondered where he had gone and why. Before she could worry too much, she saw him walking toward her through the trees and foliage. Naledi was relieved to see him. As he moved closer, she could see he held more fruits and berries in his hands. She grinned as he brought them both a good breakfast. The two of them sat under a tree for shade and slowly ate their breakfast together. They ate in silence occasionally looking over at one and another. Aldo tossed the skin of his last banana aside and then stood up tall. He looked over his shoulder down at Naledi Looking up at Aldo. She took the last bite of her breakfast tossed the remains away. She slowly stood up her knees ached as she lifted herself off the ground. Standing up she stepped forward beside her new friend. Aldo led the way as they began the day's journey.

Caleb rubbed his sore injured head. He stood up and walked among his downed men. He tried his best to rally them. They were difficult to waken. They had been severely beaten. After a couple of hours Caleb got his men up and slowly moving, as he followed the path before him. He hoped he could eventually catch up with the woman and her man-creature friend. He wanted desperately to kill them both. He had to think of a plan how to do that if he ever caught up with them again. That was going to be difficult he lost his pistol and the element of surprise, also the man-creature was incredibly strong.

Aldo pushed his way through the jungle. Naledi followed close behind him. She followed Aldo close enough to be his shadow. She wondered where he was going, where he was leading her. She walked a couple steps behind Aldo. Many thoughts and questions ran rapidly through Naledi's mind as she walked behind Aldo. Most of her thoughts were about Frank, Greg and the crew of the boat. She had no answers to her many questions, "Where was the crew now? Were they ok or injured? Had Aldo seen them? Might he know where they were?" These and many more questions ran endlessly through her mind. She hoped soon she might find some answers, but she was not so confident she would find any answers. Except for the great help of her new friend Aldo, she was on her own.

Despite Aldo's efforts clearing a path through the jungle Naledi still felt the heat of the day rising. Sweat was cascading down her forehead and seeping into her eyes Her eyes itched and burned as sweat leaked into her eyes. She tried rubbing her eyes, but her hands were slick with sweat too. Wiping sweat away gave her no relief. She wished she had towel or any clean cloth to wipe her face and eyes clean and remove the irritation she felt. She tried blinking a lot and letting her eyes cry to wash away the irritation in her eyes, but to no avail. In desperation she wandered to the stream beside her. First, she stuck her face in the water, she very briefly worried about possibility of parasites. She took a long drink. Then she sat up and splashed water on her face. She felt cooler which was a relief. She blinked several times. The irritation slowly subsided. Naledi stood up and walked back behind Aldo. She noticed Aldo looking over at her as she approached. She was not certain, but the expression on his face looked like one of concern. She began to follow Aldo as she had been doing before.

Caleb urged his men to follow him. They began to line up behind him and resume their pursuit of Naledi. One man, Phillipe, stayed where he was. He did not move. Caleb shouted at him "Come on We need to get moving." "No!" Phillipe angrily replied. Caleb was furious "Get moving. We need to catch the woman and kill her." No, she is protected by that beast. Did you not see what it did to us. I am lucky it didn't kill me. My arm is broken. I am not going to risk my life again. He protested. He sat down under a tree and stayed still in defiance. "Fine after I will kill them first, then I will come back and kill you." Threatened Caleb.

Caleb stormed off leading his other teammate after his prey. He had no difficulty following them. The path Aldo cleared through the jungle was easy to follow. With such a clear and obvious pathway Caleb hoped to catch up with the woman soon. His man plodded along slowly behind him. He was frustrated by his man's slow progress and persistent complaining. Still Caleb followed the pathway cut through the jungle vegetation. He was grateful the path was so easy to follow. It did not require tracking skills the path in front of him was noticeably clear. Anyone could follow it with ease.

Naledi waved her hand in front of her face as she walked, she tried in a futile attempt to brush away a swam of gnats swirling around her head. Swatting at them did not cause the clouds of gnats to disperse nor was she lucky enough to hit any of them either. The annoyance of the gnats distracted her from noticing the tiny flying bugs that were biting at her exposed skin of her arms and legs. She watched Aldo scope up handfuls of mud from the bottom of the stream. He carried mud and water dripping from his hands as he stepped up to where Naledi sat. He leaned over her and began rubbing mud over her bare arms. She wondered why he was doing this. She did not like the mud spread over her arms and exposed skin. She especially did not like it spread over the back of her neck, cheeks, and forehead. It was uncomfortable and made her feel so very dirty. The mud started to itch as it dried, but she eventually realized the mud was keeping biting insects off her body for that she was grateful.

About noon the two of them sat under a tree eating their usual meal of bananas and berries. While Naledi was grateful as always for the food Aldo provided for them. She desperately craved a big juicy Cheeseburger preferably with grilled onions. As she ate another banana, she knew such a craving was now impossible to satisfy.

Caleb continued to follow the path ahead of him. It was difficult to keep his man following along with him. His man was moaning and groaning with each step taken. Caleb was frustrated and annoyed by his consistent moaning and whining. He was not without his own aches and pains as he walked, but he did not moan and complain about it.

Caleb looked at his surroundings as he pursued the woman and man-beast. He was surprised by how familiar the surroundings were becoming, could they possibly be headed to where he thought he was headed? He found it difficult to believe the direction he was now headed was the destination of his prey as well. That would be too convenient.

Naledi stayed close behind Aldo. She thought he was beginning to slow his pace down. As she watched Aldo it seemed to her that he was being more cautious as they moved forward. Was he afraid of something? She did not think that possible of her giant friend. It became clear as they moved forward Aldo was on the alert for some potential danger, she could not imagine what could be a danger to her herculean friend. Aldo slowly moved a little further ahead then came to a stop behind some thick bushes. Naledi moved up next to him behind a palm tree. Aldo waved his hand up and down with his fingers pointing to the ground. He crouched down as low as his large size would allow him to do. Naledi followed his signal and crouched low behind the tree. She poked her head around the tree in an attempt to see what was in front of them that made Aldo so overly cautious. It was difficult to see past her huge friend. It took a lot of patience and maneuvering herself to get a better view. Naledi finally thought she saw something just beyond them. To her it looked like a brick wall possibly of a building. If it were a building maybe she could find help there and possibly a way off the island. Naledi stood up. She began to jog toward the building. She hoped she could find a telephone or radio there to call for help and get off the island. As she dashed forward Naledi felt a strong painful pull on her arm pulling her backward and stopping her progress there was a strong pain in her shoulder. She looked up. Aldo was staring harshly down at her shaking his head "NO" He had a tight vise-like grip of her arm. Naledi looked up at him bewildered. Aldo had never hurt her before, and he had done so much to protect and care for her. This behavior was unexpected and baffling. Why had he stopped her and so roughly? Aldo carefully pulled her down with him undercover behind the tree. The strength of Aldo's grip on her arm told her there must be something he feared here. She could not image what could possibly make someone as big and strong as Aldo afraid.

Caleb moved forward. He barked orders urging his man to follow him. He was now in familiar territory. He was gaining advantage with each step. He was now on his terrain. He felt a growing sense of home field advantage moving forward. He tried to encourage his teammate, but he was moving slow and still aching from the violent beating he had taken earlier. Now that he could see his enemy, he began edging his way closer to the beast. As he moved cautiously forward. He worried that the foliage under his feet might create sounds signaling his approach. Any sound of his movement through the jungle could lose him the element of surprise making it near impossible to kill the beast. Each step Caleb took was done slowly and with deliberate precision. It took him several minutes to get within striking distance of the monster. He raised his arm and swung as hard as he could. He struck Aldo hard on his head with a rock. Aldo staggered slightly. He was a bit dazed. Aldo growled in shock and pain. Naledi turned toward Aldo to see what was happening. She saw Aldo hold his head in pain. She also saw Caleb raise his arm to strike again. She could not let that happen. She ran toward Aldo. As Caleb prepared to strike again Naledi put herself between him and Aldo. Caleb swung his arm forcefully at Aldo. Naledi grabbed at his arm. She missed, but she diverted his attack. He failed to hit Aldo again because of her interference. Instead, he stuck Naledi hard on her shoulder. She felt intense pain in her shoulder.

Aldo had regained his composure. He reached out and grabbed Caleb's arm. He gave it a strong twist. Caleb dropped the rock. Aldo picked it up and slammed it against his head. Aldo was extremely angry. He struck Caleb in the head repeatedly. Caleb collapsed into unconsciousness. At the sight of Caleb's defeat his other man turned and hastily retreated. He quickly ran out of sight not wanting to confront Aldo again.

Aldo knelt beside a collapsed Naledi. She clutched her shoulder in pain. She soon learned that she had broken her clavicle. Aldo stroked her hair in sympathy he did not know what else to do. So, he cuddled her and held her close to him. Naledi clutched her aching shoulder. She looked down at their assailant sprawled motionless on the ground. She wondered if he was just unconscious or much worse. She got to her feet and resumed walking toward the building. She had moved just a few steps when she felt huge furry arms embrace her around her waist and lift her feet off the ground. Aldo held her firmly and pulled her back toward the trees. She looked up at him. He glared sternly down at her as he carried her away to safer ground. Aldo set her gently under the trees then he sat down beside her. Naledi looked up at Aldo then pointed toward the building. Aldo frowned and vigorously shook his he "No." He was clearly opposed moving toward the building. Naledi again pointed in the direction of the building. Aldo gripped her around her wrist pulling her hand away while shaking his head" No." Naledi tried to explain to him why she wanted to get into the building. It was unclear if he understood what she was saying, but his opposition to her plan was unmistakable.

She rested in his arms. Relaxing against Aldo was comforting. Her shoulder throbbed in pain. Resting in his arms helped ease her pain. As the afternoon began to give way to evening. Naledi fell asleep after the excitement of the day in Aldo's arms. Aldo looked over her and slowly stroked her hair. He eventually fell asleep too. Aldo enjoyed having this strange young woman as a friend. He had been alone on his own for so many months it was a pleasure to have a friend and a pretty one at that.

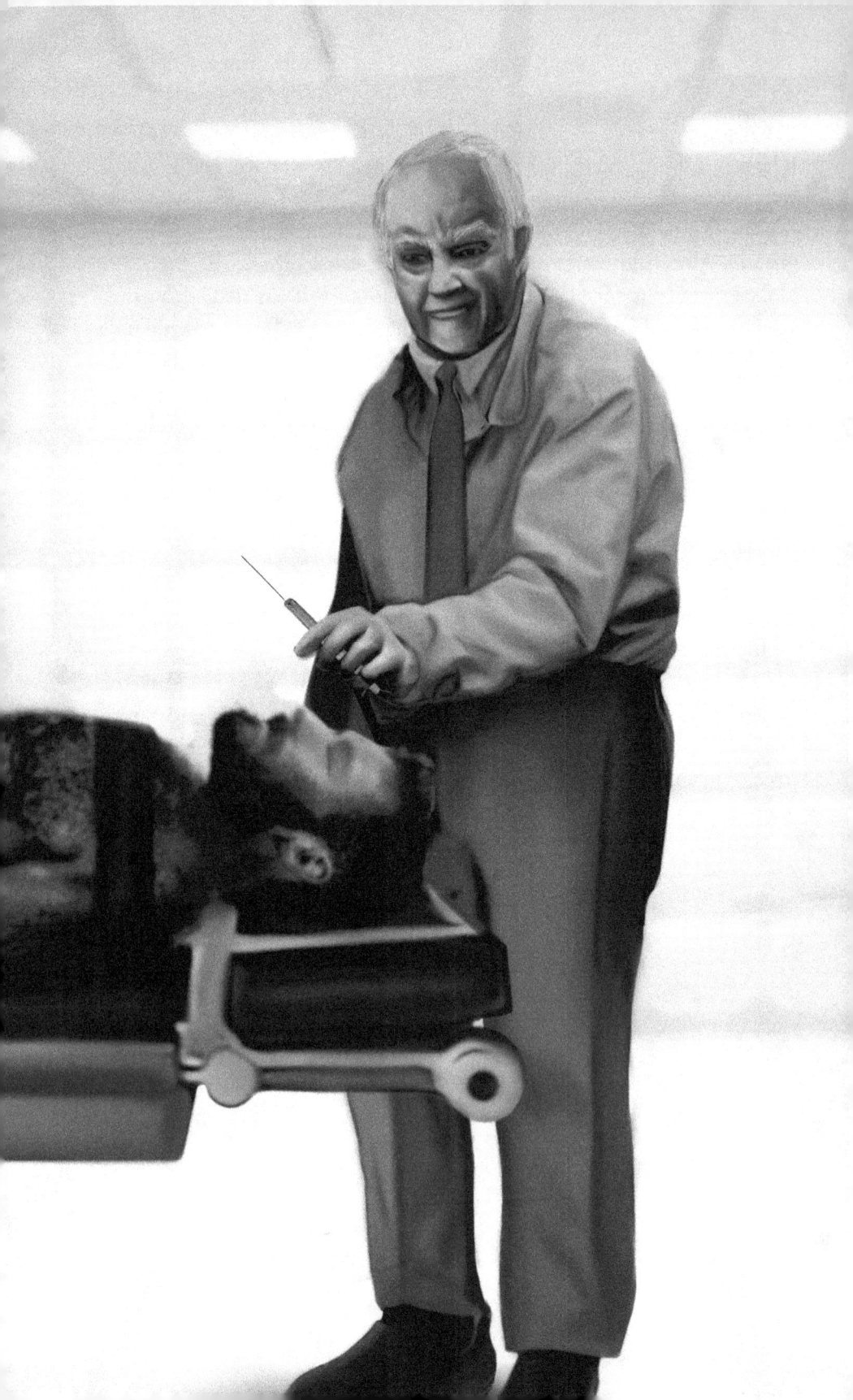

CHAPTER 5
THE LAB

In the early hours of the morning Naledi woke up. She sat in Aldo's lap enfolded in his arms. She gazed up at him. She saw he was deep asleep. She carefully lifted his arm off her and slipped out of his embrace. She slowly stood up away from him. Naledi hated to deceive her friend, but she had to see if there was a way to call for help within the building. She desperately wanted off the island. If she stayed on the island, she was afraid she would not survive. She left Aldo behind and began moving toward the building. She crouched down as she reached the edge of the jungle. She was in unfamiliar territory, but she had the benefit of moonlight to see by. Beyond the edge of the jungle there was several yards of flat open terrain between Naledi and the building.

Staying as low as she could Naledi scurried across the open space. At the building resting on her knees, she saw no point of entry. On her hands and knees, she crawled looking for a way in. It took several minutes of crawling, but finally she spotted a door. She reached up for the latch just above her. Gently she pulled down on the handle. She leaned her uninjured shoulder against the door and cautiously eased it open. She pushed the door open and crawled inside. Her eyes adjusted to the dim moonlit room. She scanned the space in front of her. Directly in front of her was a bare entryway. She crawled across the tiled floor. The entryway opened into a large room. At the entrance to the room Naledi could see the illuminated panels of several large machines. Being cautious and taking Aldo's fears seriously She crawled behind one of the machines from her hiding spot she peered around at all the machines and technical equipment in the room. Some of it she recognized. A lot she did not know what it was. It was clear to her that much of the equipment was all for genetics research and manipulation. There were also several large computers for fast computations of large volumes of data. She wondered why it was all here and for what was it being used. Many ideas raced through her mind. Most of the ideas that ran through her mind were not good ones. Staying hidden behind the machines she slowly crawled across the room. She studied each machine carefully as she passed it. On the far side of the room was an open doorway. Crawling as close as she dared to the doorway, Naledi peeked into the next room. There she saw medical examining tables spread around the room. On at least a one of the tables she could see a prone figure laying there. From the edge of the doorway, she studied what she could see. Who was laying on the table she wondered. She cautiously crawled a few feet into the room. Naledi was stunned when she realized what was in front of her. Laying on the table closest to her was the unmistakable figure of Frank, the leader of this mission. She wondered if he was injured. She tried to think of any reason why he might be laying there. Before she could move much closer, she heard the shuffling of feet approaching from behind her. Naledi hid as herself as quickly as she could She ducked down low behind one of the machines. A pudgy balding silver- haired old man walked past her and up to Frank. The strange man stood beside Frank. "I see you are beginning to develop." Said the old man. Frank noticed his arm was hairier than before. He wondered why and what did it mean? "who the hell are you? Where are my men?" growled Frank. "I am Dr. Ivan Sokolov. As for your men they are no longer of any concern to me" the old man answered. "what do you mean no longer of any concern?" bellowed Frank. "I mean they cannot interfere with my work now or ever. They have been dealt with. They are less a threat to me than are you and you are going nowhere." "Do you have them imprisoned too? Frank asked. "No, that is not necessary for them" answered Dr. Sokolov. Naledi listened carefully. She feared the men were dead, as she knew she was lucky to still be alive. She cowered behind a large machine trying to stay hidden and safe. She listened to the doctor talk to and threaten Frank. Naledi did not personally like Frank, but he appeared to be the only other survivor from the ship, so he was the only person who could help her escape the island. She had to help him so they could work together to escape the island. Unfortunately, she had no idea how to free him and escape together. Dr. Sokolov Stood over Frank. "You are starting to make progress." He said. "Not as much as your friend over there but progress all the same" he continued. "Friend?" Who was he talking about Naledi wondered. Could another member of the team be alive she hoped. Frank was the only person she had seen so far. From her hiding spot she cautiously leaned out to peek. She tried to look passed Frank to the other side of the room. She had no success seeing beyond Frank and the doctor. Failing to see further she withdrew to the safety of her hiding spot. "I have other things to do, but I won't leave you alone." Said the doctor. A beast similar to Aldo stepped up behind the doctor and stood guard over the room. Dr. Sokolov said "my friend here will keep you company and make sure no one leaves the room."

From her hiding spot Naledi saw a beast similar to Aldo standing behind Dr. Sokolov. The beast looked like Aldo, but she sensed no empathy in him just anger and hatred. Naledi feared this beast she withdrew further into her hiding spot. She curled up into her hiding place.

Naledi wondered how to free Frank and escape with the beast standing guard. She knew her chances of freeing Frank were not good. She began trying to think up a plan. Carefully and quietly, she pulled some scalpels off a nearby desk. She grabbed a few items off the desk and threw them across the room. The items clattered on the other side of the room. The beast turned his head and took a few steps toward the direction of the sound. The beast was distracted by the sound just as Naledi had hoped. She quickly moved to Frank and tried to hastily cut him free. Naledi cut away at Frank's restraints with a scalpel. She frantically sawed against his restrains. She was relieved when his bindings finally were cut through.

Naledi ducked back into hiding as soon as she cut through Frank's restraints. She was relieved to be back undercover. A moment later Dr. Sokolov stepped back into the room. "what's going on?" he questioned Frank. He looked over at Frank carefully. "you won't get free. Even in the unlikely chance you slip out of your bindings. My friend here..." The doctor pointed at the dark-haired monster." ... Will make sure you don't escape."The doctor glared menacingly at Frank as if daring him to try to escape. Frank laid very still. He did not want to reveal that his bonds had been cut. Naledi had been watching the scene carefully. She hoped

Frank would stay safe. The doctor turned to leave again. "I leave you in my guardian's care." He said as the doctor again pointed at the dark-haired monster.

Naledi was surprised by the sound of heavy footsteps behind her. Had she been discovered? Was another mercenary sneaking up behind her? She turned around to see a familiar large furry form approaching her. She was surprised but pleased to see Aldo stood firmly alongside her. Dr. Sokolov turned to face Aldo. "Well, Well. Look who has decided to show up." Declared Dr. Sokolov. The doctor stared at Aldo from a few feet away. "My, my you have made a lot of improvement." Said the doctor. He looked slowly up and down at Aldo. Aldo growled at him." "What's the matter are you not happy with the progress you have made?" the doctor continued. Aldo growled louder as the dark beast stepped up beside the doctor. "How strong are you? Now we will see." the doctor teased Aldo. The dark-haired beast growled back at Aldo while flexing his muscles. While the doctor concentrated on Aldo Naledi crawled quietly toward Frank. Frank told Naledi to go back into hiding. Frank stood his ground preparing to go on the defensive. The dark- haired beast growled and rushed Aldo. The beast grabbed Aldo around his chest. Aldo grabbed the beast. Naledi hid behind one of the machines as she had done earlier. From there she looked over at her friend Aldo. She saw the other beast wrestle with Aldo. A brief expression of shock crossed Aldo's face. Naledi screamed as the huge fight began. The doctor turned toward the sound of the scream. He realized someone else was in the room, possibly a woman. He grinned he had never had a female test subject, which opened many new and interesting possibilities. Naledi was worried Aldo would be hurt or worse. Frank kneeled down beside Naledi as together they watched Aldo and the beast fight.

Frank grabbed some bladed tools off a nearby desk.

Aldo groaned as the beast squeezed his chest tightly. As he groaned Aldo's breath escaped his lungs. He struggled against the beast, which was stronger than him. Frank saw Aldo struggling. He could not let the beast win. Frank moved up behind the beast, as the fight continued. Frank took a knife in his hand and attacked the beast. He moved up behind the beast. He slashed the beast behind his knee cutting deep through muscles and tendons. The beast lost his balance as his knee became suddenly weak. Aldo broke the beast's hold. Aldo punched the beast hard in the face as it collapsed to the floor. Frank went back into hiding with Naledi. The noise and commotion brought a curious Dr. Sokolov back into the room. The doctor was stunned to see his beast and servant laying helpless on the floor with a large stream of blood flowing from his leg. Looking up across the room he was equally shocked to see his prisoner Frank was missing. Frank looked suspiciously over at Aldo. He held his knife out in front of him Naledi shouted over at Frank. "Don't hurt him. He is my friend, and he saved my life." Frank lowered his knife. Frank then looked from Aldo to Naledi and back again. Naledi stood up and rushed over to Aldo and gave him a big hug. She stood between Aldo and Frank. Frank stood his ground staring at them both. "This is Aldo. He is my friend." Frank looked at her "I understand, but he looks like the other beast, except for the color of his hair." "He is not your enemy, that doctor is." Naledi Answered. Frank turned his attention to Dr. Sokolov, who just re-entered the room. Aldo, Frank and Naledi turned to face Dr. Sokolov. The doctor was holding and pointing a small hand handheld crossbow. He pointed it at Aldo then he redirected his aim at Frank. Aldo took a large step toward the doctor. Aldo leaned forward and forcefully slapped the crossbow out of the doctor's hand. He then punched the doctor hard in the face. Then the doctor collapsed. He fell to the floor after feeling the strength of Aldo's fist. Frank's opinion about Aldo began to change as he saw him knock the doctor to the floor. Frank grinned up at Aldo. "Now that he has been taken care of here, we should leave and get out of this place." Naledi said as she looked over at Frank and Aldo. "I can't leave yet" replied Frank. "Why?" asked Naledi. "There maybe some of my men in here." Frank answered. Frank wandered slowly through the room he had been strapped down in. As he walked toward the other side of the room, he saw someone else strapped down to a lab table. He noticed IV bags and tubes next to the table. Frank could not recognize who lay on the table. At a short distance it looked like another beast to Frank. It was not until he stood over the individual on the table that he recognized it was Greg laying helpless on the table. Naledi stepped toward Frank and handed him the pistol that had been confiscated from her pursuers. Frank stared at Naledi and screamed "You had this all the time? I could have used it earlier." "I don't think it has many bullets left and I didn't want the noise to alert other guards or henchmen." Naledi replied defensively. Aldo picked up paper and a clipboard from nearby desks Naledi watched with fascination as Aldo scavenged through the desks. What was he after and looking for she thought. Within a few minutes his purpose revealed itself. With blank pages attached to the clipboard he picked up a pen and slowly began to write. Aldo picked up a pen and began to write. Naledi was very curious as she watched him. She wondered what he was writing. All she could tell was he seemed very intent on whatever he was writing. Meanwhile Frank cut Greg loose and helped him to stand up. Greg leaned on Frank for support he was quite weak. Greg dragged his feet as he attempted to walk with Frank's support. Frank guided Greg back to where he left the others. Naledi turned her attention away from Aldo to Greg as she heard the loud sound of his shuffling feet as Frank pulled him into the room. Naledi wondered who was with Frank. She could not recognize who he was assisting to walk toward her and Aldo. Aldo did not notice he was busy writing on the clipboard. The strange individual leaning on Frank's shoulder began to look vaguely familiar as they got closer. There was something in the face of the individual who leaned on Frank's shoulder that started to remind Naledi of someone, but who she had no idea. Frank set down Greg in a chair where he could rest. Frank looked up at Naledi and told her to get some food and water for Greg. Naledi hurried off to search for food and water. In another room she found cupboards filled with non-perishable food stock. She pulled several cups off a shelf and filled them with water from a kitchen faucet. She put the cups of water all on a tray she found. She also put lots of crackers, a can of mixed nuts and a few cans of fruit and canned meats on the tray. She returned with food and water for not only Greg, but everyone. Naledi brought the food and cups of water back to everyone. Then she looked around for a can opener. She found one within a few minutes She sat down and began eating a can of pears after delivering everything to her comrades. Frank and Greg were engaged in conversation. Naledi wanted to leave this place. Aldo sat by Naledi as he began eating a packet of Tuna. Aldo smiled at Naledi, but his smile was not easy to see under all his hair. Naledi wondered what Dr. Sokolov had been doing here. She thought the answer must be here somewhere. After she finished eating her pears. She stood up and began to walk looking around. She searched for evidence of what the doctor had been doing. She searched the desk shelves and drawers for more information. After opening every drawer, filing cabinet and shelf she uncovered documents, notebooks, and notepads. It all contained detailed complicated information. It would take her a long time to read it all and even longer to decipher. She studied the documents and notebooks carefully. She did her best to make sense of them. She sat down near Aldo and began reading through the information she had gathered. It was difficult for her to make sense of what she was reading, but it was clear to her that the doctor had been conducting some form of genetic research and experimentation. She paused reading all the technical notes and journals. She picked up a small stack of handwritten papers. Holding the papers Naledi realized the papers had recently been written by Aldo. Now, she had a chance to learn more about her new friend. After a few paragraphs Naledi began to cry as she learned who Aldo had been, what he had lost and what the evil doctor had done to him. She learned that Aldo had been a local fisherman. He had been captured by Dr. Sokolov's henchmen. After being captured he had become one of the doctor's experimental subjects. It was clear he had been a good man with a young family before he had been turned into the creature he now was. Once he turned into a strange beast. As he transformed into an animal, he lost his family and his humanness. She felt much more sympathetic and cared more deeply about Aldo after all she had read. After talking with Greg, Frank started looking around for some way to contact the world outside of the island. He wanted to call for reinforcements and transportation off the island.

Frank did not find any telephone or radio, but he did find a laptop. He opened the laptop he wrote an email and sent it to everyone he could think of. His email was an urgent call for help and a ride off the island. After he sent his message, Frank searched the laptop for any information and evidence of the doctor's activities. During the search he noticed a lot of internet activity including data uploads to a cloud server. Frank unplugged the laptop and took it with him. He needed computer experts to do a more thorough search than what he could accomplish. Frank walked back to where Naledi and Aldo were. Naledi asked Frank if he got a message out to call for help. She noticed the laptop slug under Frank's arm. "I have his PC, it will have a lot of his data.," replied Frank. "I need to get it back so computer technicians can search and decipher the data on it. I can't do it myself. Maybe the data can lead to a cure for Greg and me."

Frank asked Greg "What happened? What do you remember?" Greg replied "I followed Hank and Bill into the dense part of the jungle. It was very hard to see through the dark at that time of night. Later I heard a shout of pain, I don't know if it was Bill or Hank. Me and other team members went to help. Something hit me hard that is all I remember until you pulled me out." Greg looked a little pale and disheveled. Greg ate a few bananas. Everyone ate and drank while resting. Frank said "we need to get moving soon. We can't stay here." As he said this, he retrieved the laptop. After they ate Frank began to lead them all away from the building. They reentered the jungle. Frank explained they needed to return where the boat was. Naledi asked why since the boat had been burned and it's remains sank. Frank explained that was where a rescue ship would look for them since he transmitted their GPS location almost the moment they arrived at the island. So, it was the first place a rescue vessel would look for them. They began their long hike together to where their journey had begun. Naledi tried to remember the path she had taken and now traveled it in reverse. Aldo and Naledi led Frank and Greg backwards along the path they had traveled together. The sun would begin to set within a couple of hours. They soon would have to camp for the night. Soon they all set down to rest in the shade of some trees. Frank did not sit down. He could not his mind was alert, and his nerves were on edge. He nervously stood guard. He was determined not to be surprised again. There was no way he was going to allow himself to be taken captive again.

Caleb woke up. He was sore all over. He felt pain throughout his body. Slowly he walked toward the building. He entered the building. It was quiet inside. He saw no sign of the doctor or anyone in the building. The further he walked throughout the building he was sure something was wrong. There was evidence of a struggle. He walked into the lab; the two subjects were missing, and he saw the dead beast laying on the floor in a large puddle of blood. Something was wrong. He saw something happened the doctor was down his patients were missing. He knelt down beside the doctor and tried to revive him. After a few minutes Dr. Sokolov regained consciousness. It took a couple minutes more for him to regain his senses. He thought about what had happened just before he blacked out. He looked up at Caleb. The doctor began to shout at Caleb excitedly. "Get them! Get them! They stole my computer. I need my data; I need my research. Get them." the doctor shouted. Caleb stared at him. He then escorted him into a chair before hurrying out of the building in pursuit of his new quarry. He was angry and wanted revenge. There were several tracks he noticed in the soil exiting the building. He tried to make sense of the tracks. Two sets of tracks he was familiar with he had been follow them for more than a day. He knew he had to be careful he was following four individuals, of which one was huge, strong, and dangerous. He would have no difficulty following them. His problem would be what if anything to do when he caught up with them. He would decide what to do when he caught up with them. For now, Caleb concentrated solely following them. He followed their tracks. Carefully he pursued his quarry. Along the way he looked for any potential weapon. He hoped he might find a dropped or discarded gun, but that was unlikely. He needed a weapon if he were to attack the beast and a group that outnumbered him, even then victory was uncertain at best. If he was lucky, he might find members of his former team. He hiked along the tracks hoping to find something to improve his odds. Before the end of the day, he reached the rocky hillside. The rocky terrain made it difficult to follow the tracks of his quarry.

Naledi and her companions decided not to camp on the rocky terrain because there was no cover. About an hour after they reentered the jungle. Once back in the jungle they all settled down for the night. After some food and water, they set down to sleep. They all went to sleep, All except Aldo. Aldo stood guard. Aldo paced back and forth; he was full of nervous energy. Aldo walked to and frow, while looking about for any possible threat. As he walked Frank tried to sleep. He tossed back and forth. He could not sleep. He wondered if any more of his agents were alive, captured or heavily injured. Frank did not dream, instead he remembered images of being attacked and seeing members of his team severely injured and killed.

He also remembered needles, injections, and strange looking creatures. Frank got up since he was having such trouble sleeping. He walked over to Aldo and relieved him as guard. Aldo reluctantly gave in. He let Frank stand guard. Aldo was very tired. He sat down beside Naledi then slowly lay down to get some sleep. Frank paced nervously about. His eyes kept searching through the night for any potential threat. He saw none, but after what he had just been through, he was taking no chances. As he paced nervously, he kept his eyes focused on the shadows of the night. He saw nothing, but he felt there was something out there. Pacing around Frank saw nothing in the dark, but he began to hear a low growling in the distance. He turned and began to move in the direction of the sound. He moved off to investigate the sound. Aldo noticed Frank moving away. Aldo heard the sound as he got close to Frank. He recognized the sound and attempted to prevent Frank from moving toward it. Frank ignored Aldo and moved on to investigate the sound. The growl got louder the closer Frank got. After several more minutes he arrived within sight of where the growling was coming from. Frank was stunned and repulsed at the sight of his destination. He saw a huge, big cat figure chewing on a human carcass. Frank recognized the uniform on the dead body. The body being devoured was clearly one of his men. Seeing the big cat creature chewing bloody entrails made Frank very sick to his stomach. Frank bent over and threw up heavily. The cat sniffed the air then looked up at Frank. Noticing that the cat turned its attention to him. He began to move quickly away from the scene. Soon he was jogging back to the campsite. Fortunately for him the first rays of morning light began to seep over the distant horizon. Dawn was beginning to rise. Naledi woke up. She noticed Frank and Aldo were missing. She went to find them. She followed Aldo's large footprints. She met Frank moving quickly in her direction. She was surprised to see a look of fear on his face. It was so unlike Frank's macho personality. Naledi questioned Frank about what had happened. He did not want to talk, but eventually he told her everything he had heard and seen. She questioned him about the cat creature. Aldo interrupted them and encouraged them to keep moving back to the campsite. Aldo was aware the cat was following them. It had stopped chewing on the dead bodies. It sniffed the air and moved in pursuit of fresh prey. Naledi looked just past Aldo as he pushed her toward the campsite. She looked just beyond him as she moved backward, she caught a glimpse of the cat creature pursuing them.

Caleb did not enjoy waking up on the rocky ground. His back and muscles ached. He rose slowly. He looked around him. There were no signs of any tracks. After he stood up, he began to walk in the direction he had been moving before sunset. He kept moving hoping something would go in his favor for a change. Caleb kept moving along the rocky ground. After a couple of hours, he could see the edge of the jungle. Somewhere in there was his quarry. Caleb began to move faster upon seeing the jungle ahead of him. The closer he got to the jungle the faster he moved. He was out of breath as he reached the edge of the jungle. He walked a short way into the jungle forest. Caleb sat under a tree as he regained his breath and his composure. Aldo and Naledi returned to the campsite. Frank had returned ahead of them. Frank nudged Greg. He woke up, he was ready to go. Greg was anxious to get moving. He wanted to get as far away from where they started, as fast as possible. Greg desperately wanted off this island. He did not want to stay on the island one second longer than absolutely necessary. Within minutes Naledi, Frank and the others resumed the journey they began yesterday.

Caleb rested. Looking around him, he saw a long straight branch laying on the ground close to him. Looking at the piece of wood Caleb had an idea, maybe he could sharpen one end of it and create a spear. He needed a weapon, unless he luckily stumbled across a dropped gun this might be his only chance at having a weapon. He picked up the piece of wood. He began scrapping one end of it with a rough rock to sharpen the end into a sharp spear point.

Naledi and her companions began walking alongside the stream toward the beach. Frank wanted them all to be on the beach, where they could easily be found when a rescue ship arrived. Frank did not know when a ship would arrive. He sent his e-mail to multiple contacts at the department. He included the coordinates of the island. He was confident someone would read his e-mail and a rescue ship would be sent. Now, they only needed to stay together and safe until a ship arrived. He was hoping they would reach the shoreline of the island before sunset. By noon he could tell that he and his companions were still deep in the jungle as they traveled.

Dr. Sokolov was awake, but he was trying to gather his wits together and understand what his situation was. His body ached as he pulled himself up and onto his feet. He looked around him seeing the damage around him. His human specimens had escaped, disrupting his experiments. He noticed his laptop with all his data and formulas was missing. He was glad that he saved a lot of his data to a secret remote server. He began deciding what to do. He thought about whether or not he should pursue his escapees. It was probably too late, and he was not in condition to chase after them. It was probably better to move his operations and set all over again. He had made considerable progress here. He could begin again someplace else building on the progress he had made. After much thought that he decided to what to do. Dr. Sokolov began gathering up discs, flash drives, notebooks, notepads, and anything that held data of his work and experiments. He put it all in a portable wheeled suitcase. Once he packed his suitcase, he bagged some food and bottles of water. After he had everything packed, he began to walk East. He had prepared for a moment like this. He knew where he needed to go and exactly how to get there. With a bag of food and water slung over his shoulder Dr. Sokolov pulled his suitcase behind him as he exited his laboratory and started walking East.

By sunset Frank and his companions were nearing the edge of the jungle. The group sat down by the stream under a few trees. Sitting down they ate and drank their evening meal. Afterwards Naledi lay down under a tree and closed her eyes, she was very tired. Aldo sat down beside her, leaving Frank and Greg sitting together. Frank and Greg sat close together opposite a sleeping Naledi. As they sat together, they began talking about all that had happened to them since they arrived at the island. Frank questioned Greg about what he remembered about the attack and their capture. Neither of them could remember much after they were attacked. Frank tried questioning Greg about what happened to him. Frank had so few facts to go on. Despite the many questions he asked it was clear that Greg remembered no more about what had happened, between arriving at the island and escaping the evil doctor than he did.

Aldo leaned over Naledi as she slept. He wondered why he cared about this strange woman. Strange as it seemed he did care. Just when he was sure he was doomed to live a life of obscurity and loneliness as a monstrous animal. This strange attractive woman appeared. Despite his monster-like appearance she gave him compassion and empathy. She talked to him, called him by his name. She genuinely seems to care about him. She had become a friend to him, which was more than he dared hope of ever having. He liked her. He had become her friend and guardian. Aldo settled down to sleep. Shortly after Aldo laid down Greg and Frank also settled down to sleep. As everyone else began to sleep Naledi slowly woke up. She stood up and stood guard. She smiled as she looked down on Aldo. She smiled. She looked across at her companions, they appeared to be fine. Naledi then scanned her eyes around the surrounding terrain. Fortunately, she saw nothing unusual, but she remained alert for any potential threat.

Dr. Sokolov walked along the trail toward his destination. This was not easy for him with his short legs. His stride was short. This made his journey longer and more strenuous. Still, he walked onward. It was necessary to reach his goal if he were to escape. He had to escape so he could start over and continue his experiments. Dr. Sokolov was getting tired he was not use to physical exertion. He was normally a very sedentary man. He knew he did not have a long way to go, but he was still very tired. He sat down for a moment. He pulled a water bottle from his bag and began to drink and rehydrate himself. He hoped to reach his destination today, but he knew that was unlikely. He had to find a place to rest for the night. So, he laid down on a soft patch of turf near a large palm tree. Shortly after he laid down, he was quickly asleep. He slept through the night. By sunrise Dr. Sokolov woke up. He felt reinvigorated, stood up and continued his journey. He walked slowly carrying his bag and pulling his suitcase behind him. He was getting close to a small cove where his private boat was anchored. He walked up to the shoreline of the cove. He tried to decide how to get on his ship while it was anchored several yards offshore. There was no rowboat to help get him to his cargo ship. He quickly came to the realization that he would have to leave his suitcase and bag behind while he found a way to get across the water on to his ship. He sat down and pondered how to get from the beach to the ship anchored several yards out in the cove. After a short rest he looked around for something to help get him to the ship. Eventually he found a large branch. He pushed it out into the water. He clung onto the branch as it floated. He floated into the cove with the branch. As he floated, he started paddle kicking his way toward the cargo ship. As he moved closer to the ship, he saw a large dark dorsal fin appear above the surface. He stared at it and became very afraid. Dr. Sokolov had a phobia of sharks. He had accepted the fictional tales of sharks as ravenous man-eaters. He paddled and kicked faster trying to race to the ship and safety. It was only when the fin passed in front of him that he realized his fears were unnecessary. The fin belonged to a dolphin not an oceanic shark. Once he reached the cargo ship, it took him a bit of time and effort to climb onboard. He got up on his feet and walked into the cabin. He opened a cabinet and pulled out several navigational maps. Dr. Sokolov studied the maps carefully. He needed to find a place where a new laboratory could be set up quickly. It also needed to be a place where he could get new test subjects easily. There were several locations to consider, but not all were within range of the ship. Remote islands of Indonesia were good candidates, but out of range. Next, he closely studied the islands of the Philippines, South Pacific and Fijian Islands.

Through the night and into the morning Naledi stood guard. Naledi stood close to her strange new friend, Aldo. She looked down at this large furry creature. He looked like a new species of bear. However, she never knew of any type of bear to live in the Pacific. Who was Aldo? He looked like a bear, but he could write to communicate with her. Beneath the fur was clearly an intelligent mind and consciousness. She could not explain why, but she believed there was a person beneath the fur. Strangely regardless of what Aldo was, she felt a personal connection with him. Looking over him she was confused about how she felt for him. It was clear to her that Aldo had become her friend. Naledi knew she cared for Aldo. It was clear that Aldo was more than her friend, but also her defender. More than once, he had fought off those trying to harm her. Naledi knew she owed him her life. She would not have survived this long without his help.Naledi sat beside Aldo while she kept her eyes alert for any danger. As she sat on the ground resting the first rays of dawn began to leak over the horizon and through the leaves of the trees. As dawn began to rise

Naledi's companions began to waken. Within half an hour the group was awake and ready to continue their journey. They ate and drank some water. They stood up and began walking in the same direction that they had been proceeding for more than a day. As they resumed their journey. Caleb woke up and resumed his pursuit of the group by mid-morning, he quickly followed their trail. Caleb was only a few hours behind them. He moved as quickly as possible. He wanted to catch up to his quarry as quickly as he could. Frank took the lead as he and his companions moved through the jungle toward the beach. As they moved along Greg called out. Greg pointed to bodies on the ground. It startled Frank. He stared at the motionless bodies of his former teammates. Nature and decay had begun taking over the dead bodies. Naledi tried to not look directly at the scene. She pinched her nose trying to avoid the nauseating smell of death. There was nothing that could be done for the dead, so Frank led the way past the spot and continued on their journey. Frank and his companions moved on their way. They left the scene of tragedy behind them. The jungle was getting progressively thinner as they continued to walk along. Within a few hours they reached the far limit of the jungle. The trees and vegetation had thinned greatly. The soil beneath their feet was becoming sandy. Naledi's spirits rose and those of her companions as they looked out over the beach from the edge of the jungle. They all stepped out of the jungle and started walking down the sandy slop toward the beach. Naledi stepped onto the beach. She enjoyed the soft feeling of the sand beneath her feet. The last time she was on the beach, she was in such a hurry to escape she could not enjoy the sand or any part of the beach. Her companions followed her onto the beach. As he walked onto the beach Frank looked out to the horizon and visually searched the surface of the ocean. He strenuously looked for a ship. He had no idea when a rescue ship would arrive. It was disappointing to see no sign of a ship on the ocean. Frank sat down on the sand when he saw nothing from where he stood out to the horizon. He saw nothing the sea was empty of ships. There was nothing to be seen from the beach to the far horizon. The sun was slowly setting. Naledi watched the beautiful orange glow of the sunset along the horizon.

Caleb moved through the jungle, he felt he was getting close to Naledi and her companions. Caleb was getting anxious as he closed in on his quarry.

Caleb finally reached the edge of the jungle the beach was clearly in sight now. Scanning the beach from the edge of the jungle, he saw Naledi and her companions. He had the urge to attack them, but he knew he could not do that during daylight. He needed to attack by surprise. He needed to wait util after sunset. Caleb sat down under the shade of some trees and waited for sunset. As he sat, he kept watch on Naledi and her companions before him while he planned a strategy of attack in his mind. Within hours he would attack and kill those who had ruined his position in life on the island. Many plots and plans of attack ran through Caleb's mind. Some of the plans were better than others. A few he briefly thought of were terrible.

While Caleb sat and plotted, Naledi sat in the shallow surf enjoying the ocean waves as if she were on vacation. The waves splashed over her legs and hips with each wave of a rising tide. Naledi played like a child sitting in the ocean surf. This might have seemed strange to some, but it allowed her to relax, releasing all the stress and anxiety she had been feeling the past several days. Her fear and anxiety gone she enjoyed herself. It was a great relief to be able to be so playful and carefree. She slapped her hands in the tide as she sat in the water.

Aldo smiled looking over at Naledi as she played in the rising tide like a little girl. As he watched her Aldo thought of his own children. Smiling he walked up to her the waves rolled over his furry feet. He watched her for a while than he sat down beside her. Naledi smiled up at him and splashed water at him. She giggled as she slapped water at him. She stopped giggling and looked into his eyes. She looked deep into Aldo's eyes and confessed "I read what you wrote. I am sorry for all that has happened to you." Aldo smiled at her. He growled "TThhannk Yooou, Nooot yyour fauuult." Despite his guttural growl, Naledi thought she almost understood what he was trying to say. Naledi was happy she could understand more of what he was trying to say. She was hopeful they could soon talk together. Aldo struggled to verbalize what he wanted to say. Naledi listened harder She concentrated on his every attempt at verbalization. Slowly she was beginning to interpret more of his guttural attempts at communicating with her. She smiled as she began to understand him more.

CHAPTER 6
THE DOCTOR FLEES

After looking over several maps Dr. Sokolov started the ship's engine. He steered the ship closer to shore, but he had to be careful not to get grounded on a sandbar. He had to retrieve his belongings from the beach. He found a small safety raft. He tossed it overboard near the ladder. He then pulled the cord and watched the rubber raft rapidly inflate. The doctor climbed down the ladder and then slowly stepped into the raft. He carefully sat down in the raft. Once he was in the raft, he began to paddle his way slowly to the beach. Once he reached the beach, he quickly retrieved his laptop and other possessions left on the raft. After he secured everything in the raft, he paddled his way back to the ship. He struggled for quite a time to carry his belongings up the ladder and onto the deck. Once he carried everything aboard and put it all away. The doctor stepped back up to the steering wheel. He peered over the map, he turned the wheel and navigated Southwest toward his new destination. He steered the ship out into the open ocean. He glanced back at the island as it began to fade into the distance. He was disappointed he had been forced to leave his laboratory behind. He was angry his work had been interrupted by meddling federal agents. He was angry that his work was interrupted and halted, just when he felt he was making significant progress.

Naledi and Aldo sat in the shallow water on the shoreline as they struggled to converse. They spent hours attempting to talk to each other as the afternoon began to give way to early evening. Naledi was beginning to understand Aldo's course guttural voice. The more she listened the more she understood, but there was still much of his words she could not decipher. Even though she understood more understanding what Aldo said was still a struggle. Naledi was beginning to understand who Aldo was before he was brought to the island. Despite the difficulty understanding what he was saying. She was learning about the man Aldo used to be. The more Naledi understood, the more her eyes continued to water until she was on the verge of tears. It was becoming clear to her that Aldo had been a native fisherman with a young family from a nearby island. He had been fishing when his canoe was overtaken by a ship of the doctor's henchmen. As he was pulling in his net the henchmen overpowered and kidnapped him. He was hauled away and taken to the laboratory. In the lab Aldo became one of Dr. Sokolov's experimental specimens.

Caleb looked out to the beach at the people who were to become his prey, as the day turned to late afternoon. He was getting anxious and impatient. He was tired of spending hours staying out of sight at the jungle's edge. As the sun moved lower in the sky Caleb prepared himself to attack soon. There was not much he could do but wait for sunset. Caleb worked on sharpening his handmade wooden spear. He vigorously worked on shaping his only weapon to a sharper point. His spear had rough, but deadly point. His handmade spear was very capable of maiming or killing an opponent. Caleb stayed low hidden in the jungle foliage waiting for his opportunity to attack by surprise. As much as the odds were against him, Caleb was sure he could kill all his victims if he caught them off guard and moved quickly. The sun was setting his time to act would be soon

As the light fade the adrenaline in his veins rose. Caleb crouched low he was ready and anxious to pounce on his victims. As everyone laid down to rest Frank paced about. He stood guard while always keeping one eye on the ocean in hope of seeing a ship arriving to take them all away from the island. Pacing around his eyes were more on the ocean than on the jungle.

CHAPTER 7
THE ATTACK

Caleb noticed Frank's attention was not focused on his direction. Caleb wanted to attack when it was darker, but he could not ignore that Frank's behavior provided him with an advantageous opening. When Frank turned away from Caleb as he paced Caleb leapt up to strike. He dashed from his hiding place in the jungle and dashed toward Frank. As he ran toward Frank, Caleb heard a crunch of foliage beneath his feet.

He knew he had lost his element of surprise when he heard the crunch under his feet. The sound alerted Frank, he turned toward the sound. He saw Caleb running at him with his primitive spear raised high. Caleb closed the distance between them. He lunged at Frank trying to strike him hard in the chest. Frank dodged the attack. He kicked Caleb's legs out from under him dropping him to the ground. He pulled the spear from Caleb's hand and broke it over his knee. Caleb lay face down in the sand. Frank stepped on Caleb firmly placing his foot between Caleb's shoulder blades. Caleb knew his attack had failed as he felt the pressure on his back pressing him into the sand. There was now nothing he could do since he failed. He was angry. He had wanted so much to destroy his opponents. Caleb now had no purpose or future with the doctor defeated by these meddling fools. Frank bound Caleb's legs with his own belt. He kept a close watch on his prisoner all night. Caleb struggled to free himself. His efforts were futile, and he knew it. Naledi and the others laid down on the beach to sleep. Frank stood guard as they slept and kept Caleb his prisoner. Several hours into the night Aldo woke up and relieved Frank from guard duty. He recognized Frank's prisoner. Aldo knew and hated Caleb. He was not going to give him a chance to escape. Aldo sat down on Caleb's back to keep him under control. Frank was very tired he laid down to sleep as soon as Aldo relieved him. As the sun rose both Naledi and Greg woke up. Greg looked out over the ocean to the horizon. Naledi looked over to Aldo. She was surprised to see him sitting on his prisoner. She recognized the prisoner. She was glad he was securely under Aldo's control. Greg called out he to say a ship sailing by. Caleb looked up. He recognized it as it sailed away from the island. After seeing it Caleb knew he had been abandoned. Naledi, Greg and Frank shouted and waved their arms to signal the ship, but it sailed further out to sea and away from the island. Naledi and her companions' hearts sank in disappointment as it sailed out of sight. Greg waded into the surf in the hope that he could catch something to eat. He was tired of eating only bananas and berries. Greg quickly realized he couldn't catch fish in his bare hands. After turning over a few rocks he chased some crabs through the shallow tide. After several minutes and many frustrating attempts Greg finally caught a large crab. He killed it by smashing its shell with a rock cracking the crab's shell. Next Greg spent the rest of the morning building a fire so he could cook the crab. While Greg began preparing a fire pit, Naledi and Aldo started gathering driftwood, branches and dried out foliage as fuel for the fire. They stacked up the firewood and other fuel sources. Greg worked hard to start a flame. It took time and effort to generate a flame and get a campfire started. Greg cooked the crab in the coals of the campfire. His mouth watered as the crab cooked. His companions piled more dry fuel on the fire creating lots of smoke. They were more interested in making a signal fire than cooking. A smoke plume large enough could signal a ship, so they could get rescued. As the fire grew Greg watched his crab cook. His mouth watered as he anticipated dining on his catch. He wondered how long he should let it cook. He was also uncertain how he would get his diner safely out of the fire without possibly burning himself. He did not have tongs or other tool to pull the crab out of the fire, he was going to have to improvise. He got a large branch and swept his cooked crab carefully out of the fire. After it was out of the flames, he crushed the crab with a rock. Once it was cracked open, he pried the meat out of the shell and began to eat the meat. It didn't taste like a fine meal, but it was much more satisfying than more bananas. Aldo watched Greg dine on his catch. He became envious when the crab was shared with Frank. Aldo grabbed the sharp end of the shattered spear. He took the sharp end of the spear and waded into the surf to hunt. He chased fish and other sea creatures hoping to catch his own meaty meal. Fish evaded him as he waded into the surf. He stabbed wildly at the water hoping to spear a fish. His attempts were unsuccessful. Fish dashed all around him and between his legs. The fish evaded and taunted Aldo as he speared wildly at the water around him. He began to feel like a fool as he unsuccessfully hunted for a meaty meal. Every time fish escaped him, he got ever more frustrated. He growled in anger with each miss at spearing his potential prey. Naledi waded up to Aldo in attempt to calm him down. Aldo ignored his new friend. He continued splashing the water as he repeatedly tried to strike at the fish. He only started to calm down as he saw a few fish trapped between him and an outcropping of rocks. Noticing this he tried to trap them closer to the rocks. By slow strategic maneuvering, a few fish up against the rocks. He finally trapped a couple fish tightly between him and the rocks. He carefully stalked his prey. He struck as quick as he could with the spear tip. He struck quickly lancing the bigger fish roughly through its body. The fish twitched on the end of the spear point. Aldo carried the fish ashore and then bashed it dead with a rock. He skewered the fish then carefully cooked it over the fire. Naledi smiled broadly as she watched her friend proudly cook his catch. Over the fire he turned the fish slowly. After an hour of cooking, he pulled the fish from the fire and began to nibble it slowly. He pulled some meat off the bones Aldo handed a small amount of meat over to Naledi. She took the piece of fish happily. She smiled at Aldo as she ate it gladly. It was not a cheeseburger, but she enjoyed her meaty meal. For once everyone dined on something other than fruits and bananas.

Dr. Sokolov sailed out along the wide-open ocean. He was so far out he could no longer see the island he had left behind. He set the course and put the ship to sail on automatic. As he cruised over the ocean waves, he searched the galley below. As he looked through the stored supplies, he was delighted to see a recent set of backup data discs. The data on the discs were not up to date, the data was about a week old. The discs would allow him to resume his experiments without having to start all over. He thought long and hard about how he would rebuild and equip a new laboratory. It would not be easy, but he was sure it could be done. While he thought this through, the ship sailed across the vast open ocean. With so far to go very little navigation was needed. The ship only needed to stay on the same compass heading for several hours. This gave the doctor plenty of time to think everything through carefully.

Meanwhile after finishing eating her meal, Naledi sat down under a tree and began reading through the journals and documents that she had taken from the lab. Once again, she tried to make sense of it all. She was frustrated some of it she understood but the rest was a mystery to her. She felt as if she was missing something that should be obvious to her. It was as if she was overlooking obvious missing puzzle pieces. That frustrated her even more. What was she missing? Why could she not see it? It was clear to her that the doctor had been manipulating DNA. Looking at Aldo and Greg it was also obvious that he had been mixing both animal and human DNA. This much Naledi was sure of, but she could not understand Why. What was the purpose of it all she wondered. She had a vague understanding of what the doctor had been doing, but she did not understand the reason why. She sat pondering what had been done. Looking at both Greg and Aldo it was clear that the doctor had been mixing both human and animal DNA. Naledi wondered what, was the reason for mixing DNA. She could not imagine was the goal for conducting these experiments.

Aldo finished his meal. After he was done eating, he stood up and looked over at Naledi. It was obvious that his friend was deep in thought. He decided not to disturb her. So, he waded back into the surf to hunt for more fish and other prey. Hunting fish had been so difficult and frustrating Aldo concentrated on finding other sources of seafood. He began by hunting crabs, but they were as elusive as the fish. He then began to concentrate on clams, oysters, and other mollusks. They were not his preferred choice, but they were easy to catch and collect. He collected a few clams and snails. As he collected them, he noticed a spiny lobster moving close by. Slowly, carefully he stalked the lobster. He leaped forward fast and grabbed the lobster. As soon as he caught it, he bashed its head with a rock. Hitting it in the head, he killed it. Being dead it would not escape. Aldo gathered up the mollusks he caught and set aside while chasing the lobster. He carried everything he caught up the beach back to the fire pit.

Naledi flipped through the notebooks. She studied them carefully trying to understand what had been done. She started to get a headache studying the details of the experiments that had been conducted. Aldo prepared his catch for cooking over the fire. While he prepared his meal for dinner, Frank called out. Everyone looked up as they heard Frank call out. Frank pointed out to the horizon.

CHAPTER 8
THE RESCUE

Visible in the distance a dark object moved along the horizon. It was a ship that was moving toward the island. The sight of it excited everyone. They all looked toward the horizon after hearing Frank call out. Seeing the ship on the horizon, Naledi and her companions waved their arms. The ship was too far out to see them jumping up and down while waving their arms. Everyone was excited seeing the ship. They became more excited as the ship turned away from the horizon and started to move toward the island. They all cheered excitedly as the ship began to slowly sail toward them. Aldo began cooking his catch while everyone else watched the ship slowly move toward them. Aldo was the only one that was still hungry. Everyone else forgot about food while watching the ship sail at what felt like a snail's pace toward the island. The ship moved slowly away from the horizon toward the island. Naledi wished she had her binoculars as it moved closer to her. She became impatient as the ship sailed. Naledi knew the ship could not get too close to the beach the ship would the beach itself and get stuck if it got too close to the island. About a quarter mile out from the island. It dropped anchor and came to a stop. Naledi could finally see men moving around the deck. The men lowered a ladder over the side. Down the ladder a sailor scaled his way down the ladder a large package was thrown overboard in the water near the bottom of the ladder. Standing on the bottom rung the sailor pulled a cord of the package, it suddenly inflated into a large rubber raft. The sailor entered the large raft. Behind him two more sailors entered the raft. A second raft was inflated, and more sailors boarded the second raft. Once all the men were securely seated, they began to paddle the rafts toward the beach. The first raft got within a few hundred feet of the beach. When the raft was in shallow water, the men leaped over the side and pulled it up onto the beach. Within minutes the second raft was also pulled up onto the beach. Out of the first raft an ensign walked up the beach and over to meet with Frank. The handsome young ensign and Frank began to talk together. Frank's companions were escorted by the other sailors to the rafts. Frank talked for a few minutes with the ensign. As he talked with the ensign Frank briefly looked over at his companions, the rafts and the ship anchored about a quarter mile offshore. Frank was escorted to the first raft. Naledi was already sitting in the raft. Greg and Aldo had been escorted into the other raft. Once everyone was aboard the rafts, the sailors pushed the rafts off the beach and began paddling toward the ship. At the ship, a basket was lowered down the side. Naledi was guided into the basket. Once she sat down in the basket she was lifted up to the main deck of the ship. She felt a huge sense of joy and relief as she stepped onto the ship. Within the next hour the rest of her companions were also lifted up onto the ship. Meanwhile Naledi was surrounded by sailors and guided to the ship's sickbay. She was placed on an examining table. The ship's doctor began to give her complete physical a sample of her blood was taken to be tested. She sat still as the doctor examined her fully. Naledi could tell by the way he conducted himself that this doctor was not used to examining women. This fact made her uncomfortable. She tried not to show how nervous and uncomfortable she was with the doctor. After the exam was over and the results of the blood test came back, the doctor carefully explained her condition to her. He told her that she was very dehydrated and a little malnourished. That was not a surprise to her. She could have guessed as much after all she had been through. The doctor told her that beside a few scrapes, dehydration, and malnourishment she was in fine condition. Naledi left the doctor and then she had a crewman escort her to the galley, she was thirsty and hungry. Finally, she had a chance at real food and something good to drink. Naledi picked up a tray and proceeded through the serving line. She got herself a big cheeseburger with grilled onions and potato chips. She took her tray and sat down at a nearby table. She sat down between a few sailors.

Naledi ate her burger slowly, she savored every bite. It was the best meal she had in over a week. The sailors around her stared at her. While she ate Frank, and the others were being examined by the doctor. Frank was given a clean health report except, for some foreign substance in his blood. The doctor was baffled when he tried to examine Greg and Aldo. He could not understand why Greg was so furry. Greg's fur made it difficult for the doctor to examine him. The doctor looked into Greg's eyes. He saw deep brown eyes, but no whites of human eyes. This confused the doctor. The doctor had to shave a patch of Greg's arm to draw a blood sample. The blood was sent out to be closely analyzed. Greg seemed to be very healthy to the doctor, but not fully human. The doctor was pondering Greg's case when Aldo was led into the examining room. The doctor looked up at Aldo and complained "What is this thing? "I am a doctor not a veterinarian. "Aldo sat down on the examining table and stared at the doctor. The doctor was told that Aldo was a member of the rescued party. He sighed in despair and began to examine Aldo. He drew a blood sample and continued his physical examination. He had difficulty getting his stethoscope through the chest fur to listen to Aldo's heartbeat and breathing. The doctor ended the examination. He decided Aldo was in general good health, although he did not understand who or what Aldo was. Naledi sat on the bunk she had been provided. She laid back enjoying the comfort of the mattress. It was far more comfortable than anywhere she had slept in the past several days. She closed her eyes and got the best rest she had since joining this mission. After a blissful afternoon of sleep Naledi awoke. She sat up and began rereading the doctor's notes and documents. The more she read, the more she began to realize why she could not understand what the doctor had done. His work involved DNA. She worked with DNA. However, the doctor used DNA for genetic engineering purposes. That was outside her scientific expertise. Naledi worked with DNA for forensic analysis, she was not trained in genetic engineering. She understood the work with DNA, but not the genetic manipulation.

Aldo walked down the corridor after leaving the ship's doctor. Everyone moved out of his way as they saw him coming. He walked to the galley. He was hungry. When he stepped into the chow line over a dozen people left the line. The food servers hid in the kitchen. They let him help himself to anything he wanted to eat. Aldo stacked his tray with heaps of bacon, chicken, and a few fresh oranges. His tray stacked high with food Aldo sat down at a nearby table. That side of the cafeteria cleared out as he sat down. Everyone stared as Aldo aggressively ate pounds of chicken. After he consumed all the chicken on his tray, he ate bacon by the fistful. He had not had such a good meal in months. He slowly peeled and ate the oranges. Once he ate all the food on his tray, he returned for a second helping. No one told him No one stood in his way. He piled his tray with more food. This time he got a couple of cheeseburgers and a large serving of fries. Naledi was getting hungry after studying for hours. She walked to the cafeteria. She noticed the serving line was almost empty except for Aldo serving himself. She noticed almost everyone avoiding him. She quickly stepped in line behind her friend. She also grabbed cheeseburgers and fries. She poured herself a large, iced tea. She walked behind her friend and happily sat down next to him. Naledi began to eat her burger as Aldo finished his second serving. Aldo stood up and began to walk out of the room. Naledi asked him where he was going. He smiled at her and gestured that he was going to sleep. She watched him walk away. As he exited the cafeteria, people moved away from him as he approached. Naledi worried about him. As he left, she felt sad to see him go. She began to question her feelings about him. She cared for him a lot. She knew she did not care from him romantically, she thought of him more like a big brother. She slowly ate her cheeseburger, trying to enjoy every bite. As Naledi savored her burger, she watched Aldo disappear from sight. Naledi pondered her feelings for Aldo. She wondered why she felt sad for him. She assumed it was because she knew he must have suffered alone on the island for a long time. While she finished her burger, Frank set his meal down on the table and at opposite her. She looked up and saw the scowling look on his face. She asked him what was wrong. He stated his concerned about what the crazy doctor had done. He asked Naledi if she had figured out what he was doing. She told him she only partly understood what was being done. Frank asked if the madman was making a bioweapon. Naledi told him that he was not developing an infectious disease or anything like a chemical weapon. She continued to explain to Frank that the mad doctor was at work on mixing animal and human DNA. Frank began to worry if he would become affected like Greg was. Frank nervously inspected his hands and arms. He frowned seeing more hair than normal on his arms and his fingernails had grown thicker. Naledi calmly ate her fries. A sailor walked up to Frank and gave him a message. Frank was told that the ship's captain wanted to see him immediately. He walked behind the messenger as he was led up to the bridge. Frank ate the last half of his burger as he walked. Frank had reached the entrance to the bridge, by the time he finished eating his burger. The ship's captain greeted him as he entered. The captain introduced himself," Thanks for coming I'm Captain James J. Mitchell." Captain Mitchell questioned Frank about his mission and all that happened on the island. Frank explained everything he could, as the captain began debriefing Frank. He explained what he could, but he told the captain that the woman he brought with him was the only one who could describe the mad doctor's scientific experimentation. Captain Mitchell turned to an ensign and ordered him to bring Naledi to the bridge immediately. The ensign saluted and exited the bridge. Nearly half an hour later the ensign returned with Naledi behind him. The ensign led her onto the bridge and in front of the captain. The captain questioned her on what she knew about the activities of the mad doctor. She explained as best she could what she knew of the mad doctor's experiments. Naledi told the captain that the mad man was combining human and animal DNA. How he was doing this would require intensive analysis by genetic engineers and biologists. Why this experimentation was being done she could only speculate. The captain had more questions, but neither Naledi nor Frank had more answers. The captain thanked them both and told them to get some rest. They would be sailing into Honolulu harbor within the next 36 hours. Naledi almost skipped her way back to her bunk. She was thrilled at the thought of returning to Honolulu and the real world. She began daydreaming of what she would do on her return. Frank wandered off to his bunk. He felt defeated. He worried that this failed mission might ruin his career. He failed even if he did manage to escape. How could this not be a huge stain on his career. As he laid down on his bunk, he sulked over all the men he lost, and the villain was still free. Naledi wondered what would happen to her friend Aldo when they arrived in Honolulu. She worried he would be lost in the city. She returned to her quarters. She laid down on her bunk. She felt safe, secure, and contented as she closed her eyes and slowly drifted off to sleep. She was happy, she was sleeping in a bed not on unfamiliar ground. She had strange dreams as she slept. Her dreams were almost nightmares in her dreams she saw herself transforming into a creature like Aldo. In other dreams she imagined many people she knew were turning into human-animals. Naledi slept for several hours while slipping in and out of dreams. After several hours Aldo shook her shoulder. She was startled and woke up seeing him standing over her. Aldo gestured that he would like her to join him for dinner. Naledi hesitated a moment to compose herself. She slowly got up from her bed and joined Aldo. She walked just behind him as he led them both to the cafeteria. Entering the cafeteria Naledi noticed everyone step far away from Aldo as they walked in. She also noticed many people staring at her as she walked with Aldo. People moved out of their way as they stepped into the serving line. Aldo stacked his tray with as much fried Chicken and mashed potatoes as he could carry. He then gathered more food and served it onto Naledi's tray. She watched him fill her tray. Aldo led the way to a table, Naledi followed him to a nearby empty table. They sat down together. Naledi began to eat as she watched Aldo devour his food ravenously. She ate her food slowly savoring each bite. She noticed Aldo staring at her as she was eating. She wondered what he was thinking of. She quietly ate her meal. She tried not to think about his eyes being focused strongly on her. Several minutes later Frank walked in. He set his tray down at their table and sat down beside Naledi. His close presence next to her made her uncomfortable. Frank gave her some counseling. Make sure you remember every detail you can. "Why?" she asked. "Because we will get much more intensive and complete debriefing in Honolulu.," replied Frank. "They will ask us for every detail repeatedly." He continued. She stared back at him. Her concern and worrying were clearly visible in her face. She wanted to forget what happened, now she would have to relive it in detail. She set her food down. She suddenly lost her appetite. She finished her meal with her worries racing through her mind. Frank told her what to expect and be prepared for when they arrived in port. It sounded to her like she would walk off the ship and straight into an interrogation session. She finished her meal, returned her tray, and then headed back to her bed. When she returned to her bed she laid down to rest. She relaxed as best she could. She closed her eyes and was asleep in a short time. In her sleep she drifted through unsettling nightmares. In her dreams she saw herself as an unwilling nefarious genetic experiment. In those dreams she saw herself transforming into a bizarre animalistic creature. She tossed and turned as her unconscious mind traveled through her nightmares. She slept for hours.

CHAPTER 9
DEBRIEFING

In the morning she felt her shoulder being shaken. She woke up looking above her she saw a young muscular sailor. She noticed he was a member of Shore Patrol, by the "SP" on his armband and helmet. Standing over her he ordered he "Get up woman and come with me." Naledi climbed out of bed. She followed the officer as he led the way out of the room and down the corridor. It was soon clear that the ship had come to a stop. The ship was back in port. She and Frank were led off the ship. They were led into a white van with shaded windows. Frank was escorted into the passenger seat. Naledi was placed in the backseat. After she secured her seat belts the officer sat next to her escorting her. After she was seated and her escort sat beside her, she noticed Greg and Aldo were placed in the backend of the van with military escorts. Once they were placed in the van, the doors were closed, the van drove away. The van left the port as it drove off. Naledi wondered where she was being taken. Looking at the expressions of the officers around her, she did not feel like asking. They had stern very serious looks on their faces. The van drove into a large hanger. Naledi and her companions were firmly guided out of the van. Everyone was made to sit in chairs along the wall. Naledi was escorted into a room while everyone else was made to sit and wait. In the room was a large wooden desk in front of it sat in an empty chair, there was a microphone on the desk and a video camera pointed at the empty chair. On the opposite side of the desk sat a severe looking middle-aged senior officer. He held a clipboard as he looked across the room at Naledi as she was escorted into the room. She was guided to the empty chair and told to sit down. She did so. She looked across the desk at the officer as he stared at her. The officer held up his clipboard and read Naledi's personal information a loud beginning with her name, address, current occupation, and personal history. She confirmed that these facts about her were accurate. The officer then began a serious questioning about her recent adventure. Naledi began by explaining how she got assigned to the mission. Since she was just a passenger, she could not give details about the journey to the island. She described the night the ship was attacked, and Captain Putnam was killed. She was questioned about these events repeatedly. Each time she was asked for more and greater detail. She was questioned on how she escaped the attack on the ship. She wanted to forget that night, but the questioning made her relive it in detail. She described her diving off the ship and the difficult swim to the shore. She had to relive those moments as she was repeatedly questioned about her actions. She tried to describe every minute to her interrogator. Next Naledi had to explain how she survived the next few days, her decisions, and actions. Her interrogation lasted over an hour. She was intensively questioned about each day of her journey inland. After a while she finally reached the moment in her story when she met Aldo. She was repeatedly questioned about all she knew and experienced with Aldo. Naledi was intensively questioned about her communications with Aldo. She was told the interrogator would be questioning Aldo later, so he needed to know how to communicate with Aldo. After answering questions about her experience in Dr. Sokolov's laboratory and their escape, her integration was over. She was relieved after more than an hour of completing her story to be released from the room. She left the room. She looked over at her companions as she exited. She walked to the cafeteria to get something to eat and drink for her breakfast. She had nothing to eat or drink since she was woken up and then questioned long into the morning. She walked through the serving line and filled her tray with a lot of food. There were many eyes on her as she moved through the cafeteria. The sailors and ship's crew around her all stared at her as she sat alone at a table. She tried to relax by drinking a tall glass of lemonade. She sipped her lemonade while trying to put her debriefing behind her. She sat alone as she ate her breakfast. Her meal sat heavy in her empty stomach. She rubbed her belly as her stomach filled up. She worried about Aldo as she ate. She wondered how he would handle the intense questioning with his difficulty to communicate. She worried that he would get angry and frustrated as he was questioned. Frank was the next person to be questioned. He worried that he would be blamed for everything that happened. He was debriefed and questioned for a couple of hours. When questioned about it, Frank could not explain how he was defeated and captured. He felt guilty for the death of members of his team. He could not explain much because he was knocked unconscious shortly after his team was attacked. Frank was questioned about his imprisonment in the doctor's laboratory. He could not explain much about his imprisonment since he was unconscious most of the time. Later he described his rescue by Naledi and Aldo. He hated to admit that the woman, Naledi helped him to escape from the evil doctor. He hated telling his debriefers of the assistance he needed from a woman in escaping. He later described the journey of him and his comrades from the laboratory to the beach. He had to confess he didn't know what became of Dr. Sokolov. He knew his monster must have bleed to death from the deep long laceration in his leg.Frank was hungry, he had only had a glass of water so far. As Frank left the debriefing room Greg was escorted into the room.Greg sat opposite the naval intelligence officer as the debriefing interview began. Greg was angry for having to endure this intense questioning after all he had been through. There was not a great deal he could tell the officer. He didn't remember much after he and the rest of his team was attacked. What he did remember was that he was attacked, taken prisoner, experimented on before he was helped to escape. Now, for reasons he did not understand, he seemed to be transforming into some sort of animal. In his opinion the life he had previously known was over. He was no longer himself. What or who he was he didn't know, but he definitely was not the man he had once been. His anger could be heard in the way he answered questions. It was getting late in the afternoon. Greg's interview was halted for the day. He was told it would resume tomorrow morning. Greg was escorted by crewman to the cafeteria. He was very hungry. Next Aldo was escorted int the debriefing room. Aldo frowned as he entered the room. It took several minutes to convince him to sit down. He grunted as he sat while staring at the intelligence officer sitting on the other side of the desk. As the questioning began Aldo grunted and pounded his fists on the desk. The interrogator struggled to learn how to communicate with Aldo. Aldo struggled to vocalize his answers. His questioner struggled to interpret his grunting answers. For nearly an hour they frustratingly tried to communicate with Aldo with no success. Aldo thought about how he finally communicated with Naledi. He reached over and picked up a legal pad sitting next to the interviewer. He took the pad and picked up a pencil. Aldo began to write his answers to the questions. He slowly, painstakingly wrote his story. He started his story with meeting Naledi. After writing about his meeting Naledi, Aldo Wrote about his experiences until the ship rescued him and the others from the beach. Next, he was questioned about his life before he lived on the island. He wrote how he was a fisherman from a nearby island when henchmen overpowered him, kidnapped him, and made him a subject of Dr. Sokolov's experiments. The experiments altered his body and made him the creature he was now. He managed to escape the laboratory and lived alone on the island until he met Naledi. The interview and debriefing process was taking so long an aide brought in a tray of food and drinks. The officer questioning Aldo took a sandwich and a tall glass of cola. He then offered some to Aldo. Aldo took a burger and a large glass of orange juice. They both paused to eat and drink before resuming the debriefing process. After another hour of questioning Aldo was allowed to leave. It was early evening now. Aldo walked down the hall to the cafeteria. People moved out of his way as he approached. He filled a tray heavily with food. He poured himself a large glass of juice. He sat down alone. He did not see Naledi anywhere nearby, so he ate alone. He missed Naledi, his only friend, as he ate. Naledi laid on her bed. She closed her eyes and thought about what she would do after the ship returned to port in Honolulu. She looked forward to when she could return to her apartment and her job. She thought about returning to her normal life before she left on the recent adventure. After eating Aldo wandered the corridors looking for Naledi. Several minutes later he walked up to her cabin. He knocked at the door. Naledi got up from her bunk and walked over to the door. She opened the door and let Aldo inside. She let him sit next to her on her bunk. They looked at each and smiled together. She asked him how he felt. He gave a frown as his response. She asked him how his questioning went. He grunted and frowned more. He tried to talk to Naledi, but it was still difficult to understand his vocalizations. Naledi picked up a pad of paper and a large pencil. She handed them to Aldo. Even though her understanding of his attempts at talking was getting better, writing was still the best way for him to communicate with her. It was very clear to her that he missed his family and doubted he'd ever be able to return to them, especially not as the man he used to be. Naledi noticed tears in his eyes as he thought of his family. Seeing his great sadness made Naledi's eyes water strongly. She hugged him. She wanted to comfort him, but she also worried that he might be getting too emotionally attached to her. Still, he was her friend and she hated to see him in pain. She hugged him and patted his back.

Looking at his expression and reading what he was writing Naledi did her best to understand Aldo. It was becoming clear to her that he was uncertain of his future and scared of it too. He had nowhere to go. He was in a place that was very foreign to him. When they were released from the base Naledi had an apartment and a job to return to. Aldo had nowhere to go. He had no way to support himself either. His future was lonely and uncertain. It was late in the day. Naledi stretched out on her bunk, laid down and closed her eyes. As she laid out to sleep Aldo laid out to sleep on the floor beside her. It had been a long tiring day they both fell asleep rather quickly. Naledi dreamed of her apartment and her life, as it was, before her journey to the island. She wished she could return to her pervious life. She slept long and deeply. About dawn a junior officer entered her quarters, stepped passed Aldo and shook her awake. She wearily rubbed her eyes and then opened them. She was escorted to get her breakfast. Aldo followed her and her escort. After filling her tray with a lot of bacon, eggs, and hash browns. Naledi, her escort and Aldo all sat together and ate their meals. After breakfast she was escorted to a room for more debriefing and questioning. When she entered the room, she saw the same officer that questioned her yesterday. She didn't know what more she could tell him that she hadn't told him yesterday. Next to the officer she saw a middle-aged gentleman with gray temples and an id badge on a lab coat. The man held a clipboard and wore glasses. The officer introduced the man sitting beside him as Dr. Allan Grey, a doctor of genetics and an expert in genetic engineering. Naledi looked at the officer and waited for his first question. The officer said nothing. The man in the lab coat asked a few technical questions. She did her best to answer his questions, but she could not provide the detail he wanted. The information he wanted was outside her level of expertise. She kept referring him to the notes and journals that she removed from the island. After several dozen questions

Naledi looked over at the officer and asked when she could return to her apartment and normal life. He told her not any time soon. She was disappointed and not happy. "Why not?" she asked. "You are still needed." He replied. Naledi asked "Needed for what? I have answered dozens of questions. I don't know what else I could tell you." The officer answered, "I have been informed that a return mission to the island is in the planning and you are wanted for that new mission." She was shocked. She said very firmly that she did not want to go. She explained that she did not know what she could offer to a return mission. After objecting to this plan Naledi continued answering questions asked by the Dr. Grey. She could not give him much detail or additional information. She often referred Dr. Grey to the documents she removed from the laboratory. She also gave him her limited speculation based on what she read in those documents. The questioning from Dr. Grey continued well over an hour. After learning she was going to be sent back to the island not home, she answered each new question with an angry hostile attitude. The officer admonished her for not cooperating because of her negative attitude. Naledi was escorted to lunch after another hour of questioning. She filled her tray with two cheeseburgers and a large stack of fries. She sat at an empty table her escort sat at the table with her. She looked across the table at her young escort. She asked him what he knew about the return mission to the island. Unfortunately for her he knew nothing about it. She asked him who was in charge of the operation. He replied that he didn't know, but he had a guess who it was. She asked him who he thought it was. He told her that he thought it would be Commodore Carl T. Mundell. She asked why he suspected Commodore Mundell. She learned the commodore was flown here from Annapolis late last night. Naledi ate her lunch slowly to enjoy it as much as possible. After she finished her lunch, Naledi sought out more information about the return mission to the island. She returned to the officer that questioned her to ask him what he knew about the return mission to the island. She was directed to different senior officers until she was finally pointed to Commodore Mundell. She found him in a front office. Naledi met a man in his early fifties semi-bald with gray hair and a little overweight. She asked the portly middle-aged man, if he was the officer leading the mission back to the island? He stared at her through his bifocals and asked "Who are you? Why do you care?" She looked up at him and replied "My name is Naledi Lebakae. I am a specialist in genetic forensics. I left the island days ago I don't want to go back to it." The commodore said "So you are the woman I have heard so much about. I am sorry, but I need you for this mission." Naledi told him all about her previous visit to the island and how difficult it was to survive. He listened carefully without interrupting and questioning her narrative. She told him after barely surviving she had no desire to return. The commodore told her that her presence would be necessary to the success of the mission. She reminded the commodore that the ship she sailed to the island was attacked, set on fire, and sank. Commodore Mundell told her "That won't happen we will be sailing on an amphibious assault ship. No group of mercenaries could threaten the ship. You will be safe." He informed her. "you will also be able to protect yourself." He continued. Commodore Mundell called a young junior officer named Roger over to him he turned to the young man and ordered Roger to "Escort this fine young lady. Train her on the firing range, then issue her a sidearm with two additional clips." "Yes Sir!" replied Roger. "My Follow me please." He told Naledi. She followed him outside and the into another building on the base. Roger led her into a locker room He handed her a pair of protective ear coverings. She slipped on the noise cancelling headset over her head immediately after she watched Roger do the same thing. Once she had slipped her protective headset over her ears. He led her into the next room. She entered the firing range following Roger. Even through the headset she could hear the popping sound of a variety of several different firearms being shot in constant succession. Naledi was guided to an empty firing line. Once she is in position for target practice, Naledi was handed an M18 9mm semi-automatic handgun. She was taught all about that model of handgun. How to use it safely and how to aim and fire it. Roger stood behind her, he wrapped his arms around her waist, and he taught her how to aim the gun at the target. Roger held her tight helping to steady her hands as she fired her first few rounds at the bullseye target. Her first couple rounds went wide. By the third round she hit the target. She slowly improved with each round fired. By her tenth round she got close to the center of the target. She shot all 17 rounds of her ammo clip within several minutes. Roger gathered the target and scored her accuracy of her shooting practice. Her accuracy was not great, but good after the first two shots that missed. He explained the positive and negative results of each shot on the target. Roger gave her a new clip and told her to keep practicing, he would leave her alone to practice on her own, He would return later to score her shooting results. Roger saluted and then left the firing range. Naledi took aim and emptied her second clip into the new target within three minutes. The target was retrieved and scored. Roger scored the target card for her. She knew she did much better than when she started. He told her how well she performed. After he critiqued her target practice. Roger taught her how to disassemble and reassemble her pistol. Next, he taught her how to clean the pistol. While Naledi was trained to use a firearm.

The prisoner, Caleb was interrogated and questioned. Caleb was uncooperative and resistant to questioning. It was hoped that he could explain the details of Dr. Sokolov's operation and intentions. Caleb was asked many questions about who he was, what services he performed for Dr. Sokolov, what was the purpose of the doctor's experiments, where was the doctor now and much more. He remained tight lipped, refusing to answer any questions. This infuriated his interrogators.

Roger returned to the shooting range. He reviewed the results of Naledi's latest target shooting. He was pleased to see her general improvement. He showed her the target and explained to her how well she had done. Naledi was pleased with her positive review. She asked for another ammo clip and a new target to practice some more. Naledi previously hated guns. She was surprised how much she was starting to enjoy target shooting. Roger stood behind her as she prepared to shoot some more. He stood behind her and gave her more advanced targeting instructions. She continued to slowly improve. Naledi almost jumped for joy when she finally hit the bullseye. Most of her shots were close but just missed the bullseye. After a couple minutes she had emptied the clip into the target. After she fired every round into the target, Roger critiqued the results. He praised her for her continuous improvement. It was now late in the afternoon. The two of them went together to get something to eat. In the cafeteria they sat at the same table enjoying a late lunch. Naledi looked across the table at Roger. She smiled and said, "we have been together all morning, but I don't know your name." He replied "My name is Roger Kinner. I have been assigned to you. It is my job to assist and protect you." "For how long?" she asked. "for the duration of the upcoming mission or until I am reassigned." Roger answered. Naledi questioned him more "What is this upcoming mission? Why am I needed for it?" Roger explained "The main purpose is to recover any evidence that remains on the island and to recover all the stolen equipment." Naledi ate slowly as she listened to Roger. Roger continued "You are needed for your experience having been on the island." Roger told her to get some sleep since they would start out early tomorrow morning. Naledi returned her pistol to Roger. She then left the firing range to get a bit of diner before returning to her bunk. She laid down to sleep shortly after her late dinner. It was not long after she closed her eyes that she was asleep.

Caleb's questioners were frustrated by his stubborn resistance. They could get precious little information beyond his name and a few personal facts from him after hours of questioning. In exasperation they had him returned to his cell and locked him up for the night. An armed guard was posted at the door of his cell. Caleb rolled over on his bunk to sleep. Morning seemed to come swiftly as the new day began.

CHAPTER 10
THE RETURN

Naledi felt as if she had not slept long at all when Roger shook her awake just before dawn. Slowly and reluctantly Naledi sat up and got dressed. Since today she was returning to the island, she slipped off her bra while her back faced Roger and then slipped on a light short sleeve t-shirt. Next, she put on a pair of cargo shorts. Roger grinned eyeing her up and down. He had to admit she was pleasant to look at. Naledi turned and looked up at Roger. He was in full combat uniform. She laughed "Is that what you are wearing?" "Yes" he replied, "It is standard attire for a mission like this." "Okay but, I warn you, you will melt like a snowman in an oven." She told him. "dress more like me." This time she saw the big smile on his face as he looked her over. She continued "We will be in the tropics it will be 90 degrees or hotter during the day, even worse in the jungle." He walked her outside onto the base. Standing out on the base grounds behind the main building was a cargo helicopter warming up. Roger led her to the helicopter. They ducked down as they walked under the whirling blades as they approached the open side door of the copter. They boarded the helicopter together and took their seats. They were buckled into their seats. A young Marine strapped Naledi into her seat in preparation for takeoff. She glared over at Roger "So, we will have No breakfast? Are we in that much of a hurry?" she asked "Don't worry we can have a little something on the way" he replied. Roger offered her a bottle of orange juice and a variety of nutrition bars. Naledi frowned staring at the nutrition bars "You call this a breakfast?" she groaned. The helicopter powered up the blades rotated faster. A moment later the helicopter began to lift off the ground. Soon it was lifting off. Naledi looked out the window and saw the base getting smaller below her." We will be aboard the ship very soon," said Roger. She kept looking out the window hoping to see the ship.

Looking out the window she saw the ocean passing below them. She looked over at Roger and asked, "Tell me about the ship" He replied "You should see it soon. It is much bigger than the last ship you were on." A moment later she saw what looked like a small aircraft carrier below them. "We are landing on that aircraft carrier?" She asked. Roger replied "It is not an aircraft carrier. It may look like one, but it is actually the S.S. Hellbender, an Amphibious Assault Ship." Before she could ask anything more the helicopter landed on the deck of the ship. As the helicopter landed two marines approached it. After it came to a complete stop, one marine opened the sliding side door of the helicopter, the other marine stepped inside and helped unbuckle Naledi. The two marines helped guide her out of the helicopter and across the deck. Roger followed closely behind them. They all walked across the deck. One of the marines said "We are to take you to the galley to get some breakfast then up to the bridge to meet with Commodore Mundell. Roger and Naledi sat together to enjoy their breakfast. Roger ate a cheese omelet with a tall glass of milk. Naledi enjoyed a small stack of French Toast with a glass of grape juice. After they finished their meal, a young marine came up to them and escorted them up to the bridge. Commodore Mundell was on the bridge waiting for them. The commodore greeted them as they were escorted up onto the bridge. The commodore looked over at Naledi and said "You must be Miss Lebakae, the scientist. I have heard a lot about you." She replied, "Yes I am, but I don't understand why I am here?" The commodore said to her, "I would have thought that was obvious. You have been there. You can show us the way to the mad man's laboratory. You may have other information about the island that could be helpful. That is why you are here and going with us." Naledi sighed in exasperation. She looked up at Commodore Mundell and said "Okay, I understand. By now I was hoping to be back relaxing in my apartment and forgetting the past several days." Roger looked sympathetically over at her. He tried to comfort her by telling her "This mission is well manned and well equipped. It should not last long. With luck you will be back in your apartment in just over a week." The commodore added "he is correct it should not take so long. Moving and recovering all the equipment and evidence is what I expect will take the most time and labor. We will start in two days. Eat and rest up we will be there soon." The commodore called one of the marines to him. He instructed him to escort Roger and Naledi to their quarters aboard the ship. They walked across the deck. They followed the marine as he led them down a metal stairway below deck. They went down one level then two levels below deck. Stepping off the stairs they all turned left and began walking down the corridor in the direction of the stern of the ship. After going several yards down the corridor. The marine stopped in front of a metal doorway. The marine turned toward Roger "This is your cabin." The marine looked at Naledi and said, "your cabin is the next one." Naledi stepped into her cabin as the door was held open for her. She laid down on the bunk to rest. She closed her eyes trying to forget everything that had happened to her recently. After a few hours of sleep, she heard a rapping noise on her door. She sat up and rubbed her eyes. She heard Roger calling her. She asked him what he wanted. He invited her to get some dinner. She stood up and opened the door. Roger took her by the hand and walked her to the galley. They filled their trays and sat down together at a table. Roger looked across the table at Naledi. He told her his plans for their time before they reached the island. He said that it would be good time for you to continue practicing your experience with a firearm. He explained that he had planned with officers to continue her practice and gain more experience with a sidearm. She looked at him telling him how she had finished well in the firing range. Roger agreed she had done well, but he explained that was against a still not a moving target. Naledi grimaced as Roger explained his plans to her. Naledi sighed and ate her dinner. She thought about the days ahead as they ate. They finished their meal and then returned to their cabins. Once back at her cabin Naledi laid back down and returned to sleep. Naledi slept deep and long. Her rest was disrupted by an unsettling nightmare. In her nightmare she saw herself beginning to transform as had begun to happen to poor Greg. She saw thick reddish-brown hair growing up her legs and arms. She was undergoing some form of animalistic transform, but she was not turning into a bear-like creature like Aldo. Her nightmare transformation seemed to be more like an orangutan. In her dream hair continued to grow over her belly and up her chest the hair grew thick in her dream, except around her nipples. In her nightmare she felt the features of her face slowly reshape. In horror she watched as in her dream her breasts were reshaped and her nipples grew darker and longer. In her nightmare they felt full and heavy, as if she were ready to nurse an infant primate. Suddenly, there was a loud knocking on her door. She woke up startled, but thankfully the noise had rescued her from her nightmare. Naledi sat up on her bunk. She pulled out a compact mirror. Looking in it she was revealed that what had seemed so real was only a bad dream. "Come In." she said. With that the door opened and Roger stepped inside. "Did you sleep well?" he asked. She replied "No, I had a bad dream. I dreamt that I became one of those experimental creatures." Roger said "I am sorry to hear that. You look just fine as always Get yourself some breakfast and then meet me up on the deck. You need more target practice. This time with moving targets." He told her. Naledi walked down the corridor toward the galley. She began to realize how hungry she was as she walked. She sat alone as she ate her breakfast, juice, and pancakes. She ate slowly enjoying her meal, also she was in no rush to get up on deck for target practice. After finishing her pancakes, Naledi returned to the breakfast line to pick up several sausage links and more orange juice. She enjoyed the sausages, eating them slowly savoring each bite. She would not get anything this tasty on the island. About fifteen minutes after she finished her breakfast she was out standing on the deck of the ship. Roger saw her as he jogged over to Naledi. Roger looked over at her and then he said, "Follow me!" Roger gripped Naledi by her left wrist and guided her toward the stern of the ship. Approaching the rear railing Naledi saw a tall handsome well-built man that to her looked to be just a few years older than herself. The man smiled as she and Roger approached him. Roger turned to Naledi and said "Naledi allow me to introduce you to Bruce Kenton. Bruce this is agent Naledi. She will be our guide on the island Bruce is a weapons specialist. He will give you advanced firearms training and target practice. Bruce was at least a full head taller than Naledi. He smiled down at her, then said "Roger tells me you did well in the firing range on the base." "Yes, I started off slow, but I finished rather well." She boasted. "Good, we will see if you can continue doing well against moving targets." Stated Bruce. Bruce took apart the 9mm pistol in his hand. He laid the pieces of it out on the table in front of him. He gave Naledi a couple minutes to look over the pieces. He then slowly began to reassemble it explain each and every piece as he put the pistol back together. After he had reassembled the pistol, he took it apart again. Next, he had Naledi put it back together under his direction. After doing this several times, Bruce had her put it back together without his guidance. She did okay. She stumbled a little but recovered just fine. Bruce then critiqued her work. He pointed out the missteps she made and gave her a few- notes for improvement. Bruce took the pistol apart again and told her to try reassembling it again. She glared unpleasantly up at him then began putting the pieces back together again. Roger returned and watched alongside of Bruce. Naledi felt a bit nervous with both men watching her closely. The two men gave her mild praise for her improvement, then gave her notes for further improvement. She was handed a new pistol and told her to prepare for target practice.Bruce told her how to aim at a moving target. Bruce then demonstrated at skeet targets. He hit every target as they were launched into the air. His skill awed Naledi as she watched. Bruce lectured to her how to aim as he shot and hit each target. Roger handed her a pistol and told her to get ready as Bruce finished his lecture and demonstration. Naledi accepted the pistol and mentally tried to prepare herself for what she knew was coming. Bruce loaded the target launcher. "Get Ready!" called Bruce" … on the count of three." he continued. He called out "One, Two, Three!" He launched a clay target into in the air. Naledi lifted up her pistol aimed and shot at the clay target. She missed She missed on her second shot. She took a deep breath trying to calm herself down. On her third shot she hit the target, but just barely. She took more deep breaths. She gained a little bit of confidence. She aimed steadily and hit the following targets. She gained confidence with each hit. Soon she emptied her ammo clip. Bruce and Roger each gave her a new ammo clip. The target launcher was reloaded. Naledi continued target shooting. She got better as her confidence improved. As her confidence grew so did her shooting skill. The biggest surprise to Naledi was how much she was enjoying target shooting. Prior to a few days ago she had no experience with a gun. Actually, she previously hated guns. Now, she was on the deck of a naval vessel shooting at clay targets. The men were impressed with how well she was improving, and they told her so. Roger told her it was good she was doing so well because she was going to carry a sidearm on the island for her self-protection. She had successfully shot more than 30 targets by the time she emptied the third magazine of ammo. Naledi set the pistol down on the table after she shot the last round. Bruce took the pistol apart after she set it down. He had her practice reassembling it again.

She worked slowly, but she successfully rebuilt the pistol. Most of the morning had passed by it was now close to noon. Together they all took a break, walked to the galley, and got themselves some lunch. As they ate together Bruce told Naledi what they would be doing that afternoon. He told her he was going to teach her how to clean the pistol and how to fix common maintenance issues, like clearing a jam. She listened politely but was not excited about the afternoon. Roger told her they should reach the island by tomorrow morning. So, she should get a good night's sleep and then be ready to go by morning. The afternoon dragged on slowly as she learned how to fix and take care of the pistol. All afternoon under Bruce's supervision she took apart the pistol and rebuilt it. She did this over and over again all afternoon. Repeating this process dozens of times, she slowly became bored with it. It was no longer a challenge after doing it so many times. The training ended late in the afternoon. Naledi was glad it was over. Still, she was proud of what she had accomplished today in a short time. Roger handed her a tall bottle of juice. She gladly accepted it. She walked over to the railing and looked out over the ocean as they sailed through it. She removed the cap of the bottle and started gulping down juice. She was very thirsty. She relaxed watching the ocean waves. Looking out across the water had a calming effect for her. The two men escorted her into diner after she had spent over an hour watching the sunset over ocean horizon. Together they all dined on large servings of fried chicken and French fries. In a more friendly atmosphere between them, they chatted. They talked about the day's accomplishments and what they would do tomorrow. After dinner they escort Naledi back to her cabin. Roger told her that he would wake her in the morning, and she would need to be prepared to go very shortly after breakfast. Naledi acknowledged what Roger told her, then she laid down on her bunk and closed her eyes. She was thankful to have a dreamless sleep. She got good rest without any nightmares. She slept long and well, but morning still came quickly.

CHAPTER 11
BACK TO THE ISLAND

Five-thirty am arrived. Roger stepped into her cabin and gently shook her awake. She sat up on the end of her bunk. Roger walked her to breakfast. They sat together for their meal. Naledi drank her orange juice quickly. As she emptied her glass, Roger told her that they had to hurry. He set down his tray he took her by the hand and led her outside on to the deck. Naledi saw two cargo helicopters warming up as they stepped outside. The door to the cargo hold opened on the first chopper Roger led Naledi up inside. There were seats along the walls of both sides of the helicopter's hull. Naledi was guided to one seat. Roger helped buckle her in the safety straps. He made sure her straps were tight and secure. He took the seat beside her and buckled himself in. Naledi looked around the interior of the helicopter. She saw a few vehicles tied down along the center of the cargo area. As she looked around and saw Bruce walk up the cargo ramp. He walked past her and sat on the other side of Roger. A moment later several marines entered and sat along both sides of the hull. They double checked their equipment the buckled themselves in a seat. Once the helicopter was full the sound of the rotor blades revving up could easily be heard. The engines ran faster and faster as time passed. The helicopter was full of marines and equipment. The cargo door closed and was locked. A moment later the helicopter slowly rose off the deck of the s. S. Hellbender and up into the sky. Naledi could feel it rise up into the air. She knew they were on their way now. She gripped tightly on her straps for support. She was quite nervous and a bit scarred too. The flight time was short barely ten minutes long. Before she could think much about where they were going, the helicopter was landing softly on the beach. The cargo door unlocked, and the cargo ramp door opened. Everyone unbuckled their safety straps, stood up and got to work. Roger stood over Naledi and helped her out of her straps. He then took her hand and helped her up. Several marines unhooked the vehicles that were lined up down the center of the helicopter. Once the vehicles were free, they were driven out onto the beach two jeeps and a cargo truck were driven out and onto the beach. Roger held Naledi by her wrist and walked her onto the beach he walked her up to one of the jeeps. He told her to sit in the passenger seat. He sat behind the wheel in the driver's seat. Naledi stared at him. She looked around to see another cargo helicopter landing over a hundred yards behind them. She looked around the beach. Reluctantly, she could see the sunken charred remains of ship she first arrived here in. Sadly, all she could think of at the sight of it, was the poor late Captain Putnam. Naledi wiped her eyes. She looked at Roger and asked, "Why did we land here?" Roger calmly replied, "These were the coordinates we had." She remembered Frank had sent their location coordinates as soon as the ship arrived. Naledi pointed toward the sunken ship. She turned to Roger and said, "Do you see those charred sunken timbers?" Roger replied that he did see it. Naledi continued "That is all that remains of our ship and the late Captain Putnam. It is only due to quick action and good fortune that I am not still laying there for eternity." Roger looked at her with sympathy. He also felt more pride in her for her ability to survive and escape. He was beginning to learn about her and what she experienced more than by just reading a report. Roger started the jeep and drove toward the sunken ship. He parked near the sunken ship. He stepped out of the jeep and looked around. He studied the ground. He saw old tracks leading in the direction of the sunken ship. He looked in the direction of where the tracks came from. Roger drove the jeep in the direction of the tracks. He tried to drive to see and follow the tracks, while not driving over them. As he drove into the island, the other vehicles followed him. Naledi looked over at Roger asking, "What are you doing?" "I am following the tracks.," he replied." But this is not the way I went." She continued." If you're not going to use me to give directions, then what I am needed for?" She was getting confused and aggravated. They were now close to a mile into the island. Naledi heard some faint growling in the distance. She slid her pistol from her shoulder holster. The growling became more noticeable as they drove further. Roger noticed a few bodies on the ground he mentioned it to Naledi. She warned Roger to beware as she saw the bodies. He asked her why because the bodies were probably dead. She answered "They may be dead, but there are probably predators close by. We could be in danger if we get too close." It was then that Roger noticed what he thought looked like a large tiger. It was gnawing and chewing at one of the distant bodies. More growling could be heard around them the closer they drove. Another Tiger-like creature came charging toward them. It leapt at Roger as the distance between them closed. Naledi took aim as it leapt high. Naledi fired twice at the leaping creature. She hit it with a bullet to the head and another in the throat. The creature fell and landed on the hood of the jeep just short of Roger. Roger brought the jeep to a sudden stop. He stepped out of the jeep while drawing out his pistol. Naledi stepped up behind him holding her pistol out in front of her. Roger walked up to inspect the bodies on the ground. Naledi examined the body of the creature lying dead across the hood. As she inspected it closely, she began to tear up. Her tears started to flow as she realized the creature she killed was probably once a person. She could see faintly beneath the features of the tiger-creature were traces of human physical features. That knowledge made her cry openly. She was thankful of saving Roger but felt guilty of killing the creature. Roger inspected the bodies. It was clear that they were the field agents that Frank brought to the island. The bodies had been dead several days and eaten by predators. Roger gathered up the weapons, ammo, and personal possessions of the dead men. He also gathered up their ids. Commodore Mundell sat in a troop truck as it pulled out of the second helicopter and dove out onto the beach. He looked at his tablet and viewed the location signals for Roger and Naledi. He told his driver to head toward their location. The truck moved across the beach carrying a company of marines as well as the commodore. The commodore was glad that micro-transmitters had been built in the belt buckles of all his troops he had made sure that Roger and Naledi also wore transmitters. This way he could learn the location of anyone on this mission at any time. Studying Naledi's location he told the driver the way to go. Roger stepped over to Naledi. She looked up at him and wiped her eyes. He saw her eyes were quite red. It made no sense to him, what was there to cry about. Roger stepped closer to her "Are you okay?" he asked. "Yes, but I killed him." She sniffled in reply. Roger tried to reason with her "You killed the tiger, but remember it was attacking us" Naledi informed Roger "It is not a tiger, not completely." "what do you mean?" he asked. She pointed at the creature's body and asked him to take a close look at it. Naledi asked him "Have you ever seen a tiger like that? Take a close look at the nose, cheeks and other facial features Do they all look like those of a tiger?" she asked him. "Not exactly." Roger replied. Naledi continued "They look more human than feline to me. This creature used to be somebody. I didn't just kill a wild animal. I killed a person." She started to whimper as guilt filled her heart. Roger believed her, but he tried to rationalize what she told him in an effort to both comfort her and calm her down. He told her it was a bizarre mutation. How could she believe it had once been a person. She told him what she had learned of Aldo's life story before he was made a victim of the mad doctor's experiments in genetic engineering. She also told him how much Greg had changed since she first met him. She explained that Dr. Sokolov was involved in some form of genetic manipulation of people. She did not know how or why, but she was convinced that was what he had been doing. Commodore Mundell and his troops drove up as Naledi finished explaining things to Roger. The commodore asked Roger what had happened. He told him about the bodies they discovered and being attacked by the creature that lay dead across the hood of the jeep. The commodore looked over at Naledi he asked her if she shot the creature. She told him she had then wiped her nose. He looked at her critically. Roger explained to the commodore Naledi's suspicion that it had once been human. The commodore did not believe that was possible. Naledi rolled the body on its back and showed him all the non-feline features on the creature's face. He tried to rationalize its appearance the same way Roger had. Naledi countered his rationalizing with the same detailed explanations she had given to Roger. Looking over the dead creature, considering Naledi's explanation and the information he already had been given on this case. He realized this mission was far more serious than it had first appeared to be. He instructed Naledi to lead them to the laboratory. The commodore ordered his men to gather up the bodies and place them and the dead creature in body bags. The bodies were driven back to the helicopter and then flown back to the ship. The commodore instructed Naledi to lead them to the laboratory. Naledi got into the driver's seat of the jeep. Roger took the seat beside her. The commodore and his troops got into the truck as soon as it returned. Naledi started the jeep. She looked for the stream and told Roger to look for it too. They both looked for the stream. She explained to Roger that following the stream would lead them toward the laboratory. After about half an hour they found the stream. Naledi turned to follow the stream inland. As she drove, she was glad she didn't have to walk in the stream. She remembered the misery of having to remove many leeches from her legs by hand. By noon she had almost driven to the inland border of the island jungle. The trucks carrying the commodore and his troops followed closely behind her creating a small caravan. She asked Roger to get out some food and drink for them. She pulled to a stop so they could have a lunch. Roger handed her a full canteen of water and a ration package. She took a big sip of water. She drank several mouthfuls of water. She next opened her ration it was a sealed package containing a small ham and cheese sandwich. It also contained apple slices plus cheese and crackers. She ate the sandwich and drank more water. After she finished her meal, she began driving again. A few minutes later she drove out of the jungle and up onto the rocky terrain. She drove steadily up the rocky slope. At the top she could she the jungle resume at the end of the rocky terrain. She knew they were not far from the laboratory now. By jeep she guessed they were no more than an hour away. She drove through the jungle along the stream. She told Roger that they were getting close to their destination. Roger kept looking for the lab as she drove. After another half-hour they drove upon the lab. The sight of the laboratory made Naledi feel nervous. She knew she was safer than when she was last there. The memories gave her a visceral reaction to the sight of the lab. The commodore and his troops pulled up behind her. As the trucks pulled to a stop the troops leaped out and moved quickly up to the building. The commodore got out of the truck and followed his troops to the laboratory. Roger exited the jeep. He took Naledi by the hand and guided her to the building. She resisted going, but eventually went along with Roger. They entered the building. Roger looked around mentally adjusting to the layout of the room. He hoped to find additional evidence. The commodore shouted orders to the troops scurrying about to collect all the equipment and any evidence they found. He ordered one soldier to radio their precise location to a cargo helicopter and tell them to land just outside of the building. Twenty minutes later Naledi could clearly hear the helicopter landing close by. Dozens of men worked on unplugging and disconnecting all the large computers and scientific equipment. Next, they moved it all outside and into the cargo hold of the helicopter. Naledi was questioned by both Roger and the commodore where she last saw Dr. Sokolov. She told them that the last time she was him he was alive, but unconscious. She added that she had no idea where he was or could be now. The men hoped they might be able to capture him, but several days had passed since Naledi had escaped the island. A lot could have happened in that time.

Dr. Sokolov had sailed hundreds of miles. He was nearing a small group of islands that looked to him be a good place to rebuild and resume his experiments. He was glad he found a promising location because his fuel was starting to get low. He sailed around a good island trying to find a great place to land. He pulled into a small lagoon on the west side of the island. He saw a stream emptying into the lagoon. Unfortunately, it was too shallow and narrow for him to sail up it. In the lagoon he brought his boat to a stop and dropped anchor. His boat was anchored dozens of yards offshore. Being well offshore he prepared his raft overboard, so he could land on shore. The doctor placed his supplies in the raft. Next, he climbed down the ladder and sat down in the raft carefully.

The troops loaded the helicopter up with a lot of equipment from the lab. Roger and Naledi searched the lab for additional evidence. Naledi gathered up syringes, test tubes and IV bags. She gathered all the medical equipment, supplies and samples she could. She also found the dead body of the gorilla like beast sprawled out on the floor in a pool of blood. Was this body evidence? She wasn't sure. The commodore ordered the dead beast to be placed in a body bag and loaded onto the helicopter. She was not sure what she had gathered was evidence. She hoped experts could discover what the mad doctor had done, how and why? She sat at a desk and labeled everything she had collected. She wrote on the labels a description of every item. She included on each label the location, date, and time each item was collected. It took her a long time to write out all the labels. After she had labeled everything, she carefully packed them in a storage box. She handed the box to one of the men to place in the cargo hold of the helicopter. Roger found more documents and files in an adjoining office. Instead of pulling out individual files, Roger had the men remove the filing cabinets and place them in the helicopter. Roger, Naledi and the troops continued to search the building. There was not much left to find. They had cleaned the building out rather well. The commodore walked throughout the building to see if anything had been missed. He found the building was empty. The building was now an empty shell. Therwas nothing in it now, but bare floors and walls.When the commodore was satisfied everything had been done, he ordered the cargo helicopter to fly everything back to the ship. The cargo hold of the helicopter was closed and locked all the doors were sealed and locked. The helicopter lifted off and flew to the ship. Ten minutes later it landed on the deck of the S. S. Hellbender. It took over an hour to unload and properly store everything from inside the helicopter.

The commodore questioned Naledi about where the mad doctor was. She told him the same thing she had told Roger, that she had no idea where he was because she had not seen him in several days. He accepted her answer. The commodore ordered his troops to search the island for the doctor. He told everyone that he must be found and captured. The troops divided into four different squads to search the island. Each squad went in a different compass direction. The commodore assigned each squad to a direction to search. He reminded them to call him to establish a communications check with every squad. He wanted to stay in continuous contact with the squads as the search proceeded. After checking their weapons and supplies the squads headed out in their assigned directions. No sign of the doctor was seen by the squads as they began their search. The Alpha squad came up to a series of cages. It looked like a small community zoo. In these cages the men saw A Tiger, a Bear, a gorilla, a Wolf, and even a Rhinoceros. In other cages there were a few raptor birds like an Eagle, a few hawks, and a Peregrine Falcon. It was strange to find this mini zoo nearby. As they explored the area, they found aquariums containing a wide variety of amphibians and fish. The squad leader called and reported what they found to the commodore. The commodore was both shocked and mystified when he received the explanation from Alpha squad as to what they had found. He was mystified because he could not understand why there was a mini zoo on the island. What could have been the purpose of keeping such a menagerie? There must have been a purpose for it, but what could that have been? He told Naledi and Roger what the Alpha squad had uncovered. The existence of a zoo got Naledi thinking. She began to speculate in her mind the purpose of the zoo. The existence of it did not completely surprise her. The Delta squad moved in the opposite direction of Alpha squad. One of the lead soldiers of the squad was caught by surprise a bizarre creature that leapt upon him and bit deeply into his arm. He cried out in pain as fangs sunk deep into his flesh. His partner up on point aimed his rifle at the wolf-like beast and fired several rounds at it. The creature was struck by at least six bullets in the head and torso before it rolled over dead. He pushed the dead creature out of the way and the applied a tourniquet to the injured soldier's arm. The wounded soldier was carried back to the squad leader. The men reported to the squad leader what had happened. The squad leader reported to the commodore. The commodore ordered the squad leader and his men to sweep the area for any other strange creatures. He also instructed the squad to capture any creatures if possible. The wounded soldier was moved to where he could be air lifted by chopper back to the ship for medical attention. The squad moved out to search the surrounding area. Every man held out his rifle in firing position just in case they were attacked the squad leader had his men faned out in all directions. He heard shouts and sporadic gunfire after about five minutes. He called his men to report what had happened. Most had nothing to report. Three reported shooting and killing a Tiger-like creature after it charged at them. More gunfire a couple of men reported being attacked and killing a Gorilla-like creature. All the men continued their patrols. There were no more creature encounters or gunfire. The leader of Delta squad updated his report to the commodore. The commodore told him to recover and bag the bodies of the creatures and then return to the lab building. After the commodore had reports from all the squads, he ordered them all to return and prepare for extraction by helicopter back to the ship.

Soon everyone had returned and began filing into the helicopter. Roger and Naledi got aboard the helicopter too. Naledi was relieved to be leaving the island again. She had come to hate this place. The helicopter took off. Naledi was glad to see the island fade from view as the flew higher and then headed to the ship. Within twenty minutes the helicopter landed on the deck of the ship. After the they landed everyone quickly disembarked.

The commodore instructed his men to get something to eat and then to report for debriefing. Naledi went straight to her cabin for some solitude and rest. The commodore went to visit the wounded soldier in sickbay. He wanted to see how he was doing and to talk with him as well. He asked the doctor how he was doing. The doctor told the commodore the soldier was doing fine. He was only suffering from the lacerations to his right arm, but he would be fine. He started to question the soldier about the creature that attacked him. The soldier described the creature as looking like a werewolf from an old monster movie. The commodore wanted to question him more but decided not to. The commodore suddenly realized he didn't need any further description of the beast. He could always examine the corpse later. He could also examine the corpses of all the other creatures they encountered and killed. The commodore walked to where the creature corpses were stored. Entering the room, the commodore asked where the wolf-creature was. He was pointed to where the body lay. There was biological forensics specialist and a specialist in genetic engineering leaned over the body examining it closely. The commodore looked over the wolf creature. He found it hard to believe what he was seeing. Looking at the creature he understood why the soldier described it as an old movie werewolf. The creature definitely looked like a Wolf, but there was a faint hint of human features just below the thick fur.

Naledi sat on the edge of her bunk.

Naledi drank a large glass of juice. As she drank in silence, she thought about her future and wondered if it would ever return to normal.

Dr. Sokolov paddled his way to shore. The raft rode the waves onto the beach. The doctor pulled the raft further up the beach. He was quite tired. He grabbed his canteen from the raft then sat down to rest in the shade of a large palm tree. He breathed deeply while leaning his back against the tree. He opened his canteen. He lightly sipped at the scotch he had in the canteen. It tasted good and helped him relax. Sipping scotch Dr. Sokolov thought about how he could restart and continue his experiments on this island. It would not be easy, but it could possibly be done. There were geographic benefits for him on this island. Unfortunately, he lost all the equipment he had. Now, they would be close to impossible to replace. He also no longer had a team of mercenaries to work for him. On this island he had no way to connect to the internet or any cellular connection. This meant he could not access any of his financial accounts. He began to realize this island might not be the best place to restart his operation. He sipped his drink as he tried to think of a way to get the equipment, he needed to continue his experiments. After he finished his canteen of scotch, he soon fell asleep in the shade of the palm tree.

Naledi drank her milk, as she drank her cellphone rang. She answered it and heard the voice of the commodore. He requested that she join him in the morgue to examine the bodies of the dead creatures. He wanted her perspective on what these creatures were and what was the meaning of their existence. Naledi stood up and stepped away from her bed.

She walked into the corridor. She called the commodore. She told him she was on her way and then asked for the directions to the morgue. She walked slowly on her way. Soon she walked into the morgue. The commodore greeted her then asked her to examine the bodies of the creatures. She walked over to the bodies. She spent a few minutes looking at each one. She did not expect to learn much from the corpses. She had already learned so much from Aldo. She spent a few minutes at each corpse. She faked the effort. She did not see anything she could learn more than she already knew. She told the commodore she was done less than half an hour after she started. The commodore frowned. She wondered if he suspected how little effort, she had done inspecting the corpses. "It didn't take you long to examine them. Are you sure you examined them thoroughly?" The commodore asked her. "Yes, I learned what I could." Replied Naledi." Looking over these corpses did not give me much new information." She continued "What do you mean? Questioned the commodore. He was not pleased by what she was telling him. Naledi tried to explain to him that she was not experienced in doing autopsies. The commodore told her to follow him as he led her out of the morgue and down the corridor. They walked a long way down the corridor until they arrived at the commodore's cabin. His cabin was much bigger than Naledi's. It was at least fifty percent larger. The commodore sat at a desk in his cabin. He told Naledi to sit in the other chair in the room. She nervously stepped inside his cabin and sat where she was told to. The commodore looked at Naledi and said, "Relax I just wanted a chance to chat with you privately." She smiled nervously at him. She felt uncomfortable. She felt like a child who had just been sent to the principal's office and he was the principal. "So, you say you are not experienced doing autopsies, but I didn't ask you to do autopsies on those creatures." He told her. The commodore continued "What are you experienced in?" She told him her main work was in biological forensics, mostly DNA analysis of potential evidence. "I understand. I also suspect that you know more than you think you do.", the commodore commented. Naledi replied defensively "What more could I know? I told the officers back at the base everything that happened to us on the island. I told them several times as they questioned me repeatedly. What do you think I could tell you that I didn't tell them." The commodore stared at her as she spoke." The commodore told her, "You told them what you experienced, not what you learned and not what you thought." He continued "tell me what you learned and what you now believed happed on the island." Naledi still felt uncomfortable in the commodore's presence. She thought about what she could tell him and how best to explain what she suspected happened on the island. She told him it was clear that some experimental form of genetic engineering had been conducted on the island based on all the advanced equipment for working with DNA and genetics made that clear. Why these experiments were being done was unknown. How they were done also was unknown. She had some thoughts on what was trying to be achieved with the experiments, but she had no evidence to support her speculations. The commodore listened carefully and then asked her to continue. She explained that she believed that Aldo and all the creatures in the morgue were once human. She even told him that she once had a terrifying nightmare that she had been transformed into a human-creature. The commodore was more interested the more she talked. Naledi asked where Frank was, she had not seen him since the day after they escaped the island and were flown aboard the S. S. Hellbender. The commodore told her that Frank was being kept under observation after it was learned that he had an IV tube in him before he escaped the island laboratory. She told the commodore that she had learned a lot from her conversations with Aldo. The commodore stared at her in disbelief. "Do you mean the furry beast that pals around with you?" he questioned her. Naledi snapped back "Yes. And he is not a beast, he is my friend." "We tried questioning him but could not understand a word he said.," the commodore replied. Naledi explained "I believe the animalistic transformation altered his vocal cords too. Have him write his answers for you. That is how he communicated with me." The commodore thanked her for that bit of useful information. Naledi looked him in the eyes and told him he could get more information. He asked her how he could get more information on this case. She told him to find medical samples of Greg and Frank more than a week or two old. The commodore asked why that should be done. She told him that would give his investigators the chance to examine and compare their DNA before and after their mission to the island. She explained that examining their DNA could reveal what, if any changes were made to their original DNA structure. Knowing this could reveal clues to exactly what was done and why. She confessed she wished she could discover how Aldo's DNA was altered. She hoped knowing how his DNA was changed could give him hope of returning to normal. The commodore asked if reversing these experiments was possible. Naledi, she told him that it was theoretically possible, but the odds were slim. She continued to tell him reversing the process was impossible without data on what changes were made. She asked him if she could leave because she was thirsty. The commodore opened a drawer of his desk and pulled out two small glasses. Next, he pulled out a bottle of bourbon and pored some in the glasses. Naledi looked at the glasses. "Have a drink." Said the commodore. "No thank you" she replied. "I thought you were thirsty." He said."I am sorry, I hate alcohol." She explained. "I would rather some lemonade or pop from the galley." Naledi asked him when they would return to the base they started from. He told her that they should return to port in thirty-six to forty-eight hours. He then told her to get some dinner and a goodnight's sleep. Naledi left the room and headed toward the galley. She got her dinner and a tall glass of lemonade. She sat alone at a table as usual. Naledi enjoyed her dinner she ate slowly savoring her meal She drink two glasses of lemonade. After she ate, she walked to the latrine. After her stop at the latrine, she returned to her cabin. Naledi tried to sleep, but she couldn't. She kept thinking about Greg, Frank, Aldo, and everyone directly affected by the madman's experiments. She wondered if it was possible to return them to their former lives. She had her doubts it could be done, but she had a whisp of hope.

CHAPTER 12
THE DOCTOR SAILS

Dr. Sokolov woke up. Noticing the setting sun showed him that he had slept for several hours. He thought about what he should do. The first thing was to get something to eat or drink. He reached into his bag of provisions. Grabbing something to eat and drink. He dined quickly to replenish his strength. After dining he refocused his thoughts on how best to continue to his experiments. The island was geographically advantageous, but he had none of the technical equipment necessary to continue his experiments. He pondered how to get the needed equipment or gain access to it. He thought maybe he could find what he needed in Jakarta. Did he have enough fuel to get to Jakarta? The island he was on now he believed was located on the far western edge of the Micronesian islands. Even if he did have enough fuel, it would be a close call to get to Jakarta. Dr. Sokolov got his raft and rowed back to his ship. He walked into bridge area. He pulled out a few navigational maps of the southwest Pacific Ocean. He studied the maps carefully. He noticed he might not be far from New Guinea. If he sailed to New Guinea, he might be able to refuel there. That seemed like the best thing for him to do now. He raised the anchor. After the anchor was raised, he started the engine. After he plotted the course. He steered the ship away from the island and began sailing toward New Guinea. Studying the navigation map, he realized it would take a couple of days to reach New Guinea. He leaned back in a chair in front of the ship's navigation wheel and drank a cold beer. He relaxed in the chair while keeping the ship on course.

CHAPTER 13
CALEB RUNS

The flap was lifted open. The food was slid under the door. Caleb saw his dinner slid across the floor. He picked up the tray and sat on his bunk to eat his dinner. Caleb paused his thinking of a plan to escape, as he ate his dinner. He washed his hands and face after he finished his dinner. He resumed thinking how to escape. He was worried that his few opportunities to attempt an escape had already passed him by. His time was running out. He would be held in federal prison soon if he did not get away. In two days, he was to be transferred to a federal prison. There he would be held until he was put on trial for multiple felony charges. If he were convicted of several or all of the felony charges, he would spend the rest of his life in federal prison. He had to act quickly. Any escape attempt he made now, would be desperate and risky, but he had to try. He thought long and hard about what to do. He looked at his dinner and noticed the knife and fork were plastic. He was disappointed, but he didn't expect to be able to make use of the utensils in his escape attempt. A wild risky idea formed in his mind. He took the metal tray and tried to break it in half. He pressed the tray against the metal bed frame he bent it down in half then bent it back up. Over a long period of time, he repeatedly bent it in half up and down over and over again. The metal in the middle of the tray began to weaken as he kept bending it. After doing this over a few hours the tray broke in half. Caleb was happy to see that the broken edge was jagged and sharp this pleased him. He checked the broken edge. He rubbed his thumb over it. He bled. He knew it would work for his purpose as he sucked on his bleeding thumb. He wrapped his thumb with a paper napkin. He laid down to sleep. He got a few hours of sleep. He woke up and got ready to escape. Set down the broke try on the floor. He laid down on top of the tray. He got himself set by covering up the tray by laying belly first on the floor. Once he was set in place he began moaning and groaning like he was in pain. Caleb moaned loud enough so the guard outside the door would hear him. Caleb believed the overnight guard was the weakest link in the rotation of guards. It was not yet breakfast time, so the overnight guard was still on duty. Caleb increased his moaning and groaning, he included moans for help. He kept up his act of being in pain. The guard asked him what was wrong. Caleb said he felt like he was dying while continuing moaning and groaning. After several more minutes of his act, Caleb saw the door of his cell starting to open. Caleb laid still and continued to act like he was in deadly pain. The guard stepped inside. He took a couple steps toward Caleb. Caleb waited still moaning for the guard to step closer. When the guard stepped close enough, Caleb rapidly pulled the broken tray out from under him and fiercely slashed the guard's leg. The guard screamed in shock and pain. Blood flowed freely from the slashed leg. The guard fell to the floor he could not stand on his leg, it was deeply lacerated. Caleb leaped up on his feet, as the guard crashed flat on the floor. Caleb chuckled at his successful attack. He removed the guard's belt. He checked the pistol and counted how many extra ammo clips were in the belt. He put the belt on and pulled out the pistol. Caleb opened the cell door and exited. As he exited, Caleb looked back at the guard laying in a large puddle of his own blood. Chuckling he said to the guard "you better apply a tourniquet before you bleed out." Caleb closed the cell door and left down the hallway. He had escaped his cell, but he did not know where to go now. He had to plan how to escape the base and get as far away as possible. Fortunately for him the hallway was empty at this pre-dawn hour. He moved quickly down the hallway while staying alert. He moved as quietly as possible. When he found an exit he quickly quietly slipped outside. Once outside he looked around the grounds of the base. He was nervously alert as he moved across the base to find a way off the base. He wanted to find a way off quickly before he was spotted, or his absence was noticed. He saw a cargo truck preparing to leave the base. He ran unnoticed to the truck and climb in the back amidst the cargo. Laying low he stayed quiet and out of sight. The truck drove slowly and soon exited the base. Caleb did his best to get comfortable hiding in between the many cargo boxes. He looked out the rear of the truck to find a good place to jump off and run away. The truck moved along the road. The truck began to slow down. Caleb leaned out the back end to try to see what ground they were passing over. The truck was going down a remote exit ramp. He climbed out and lowered himself down from the cargo gate just holding himself off the road. As the truck passed a thick grassy median. As the truck slowed more turning with a curve in the road. Seeing a thick, overgrown knoll Caleb let go of the truck and jumped toward the thick grassy area on the shoulder of the road. He landed hard and rolled through the grass. He rolled to a stop. After a minute Caleb got to his feet, he was sore and in pain all over. He paused for a moment and checked himself for injuries. He was very fortunate that he had no broken bones. As the truck faded from sight he began to slowly walk away from the road. As he walked away from the road and thinking how much he wanted to find and kill that young black woman. He would not be in this situation if it were not for that woman and her man-beast friend. He continued to walk away and find a place to hide.

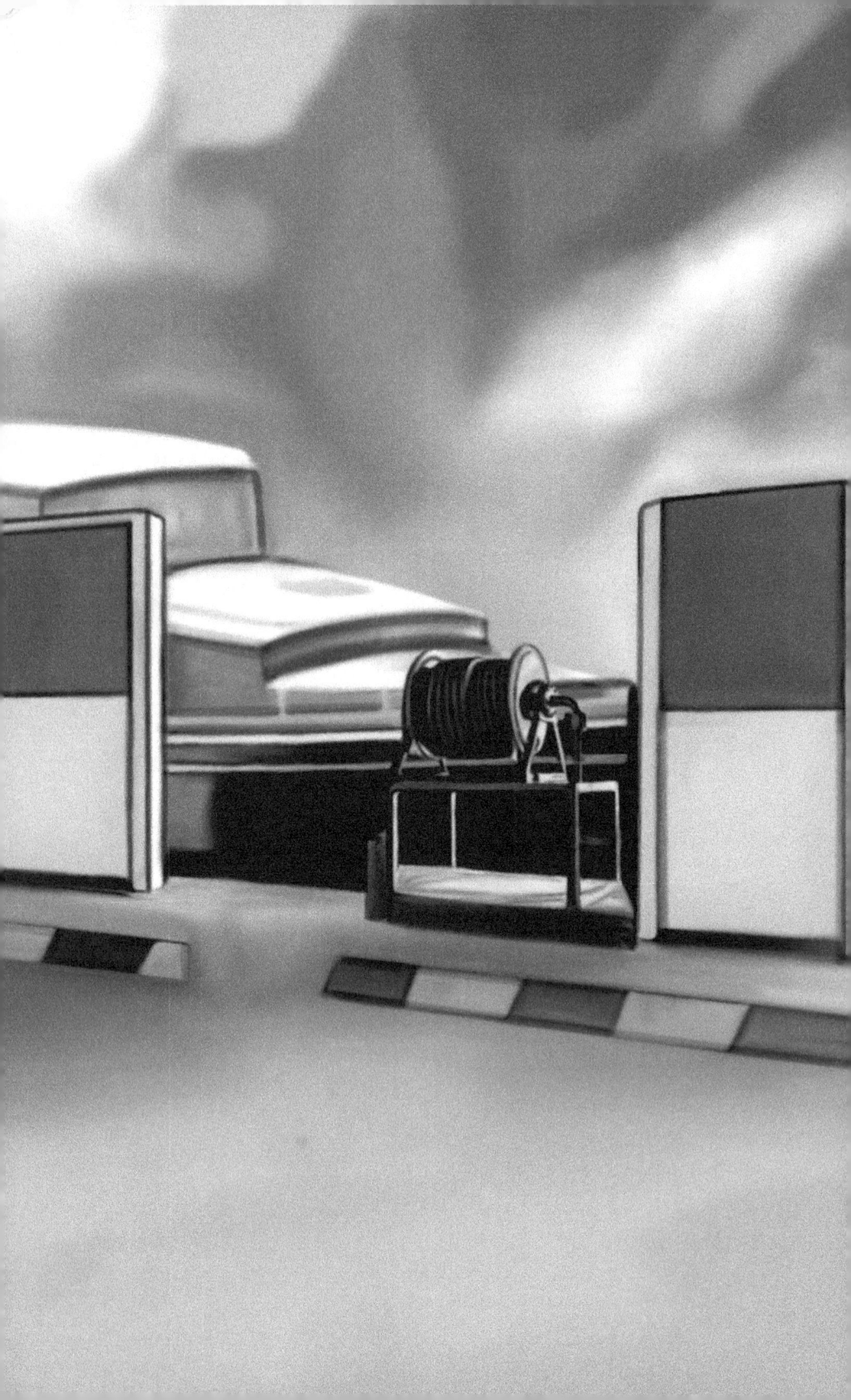

CHAPTER 14
NEW GUINEA

Dr. Sokolov sailed into a New Guinea port. He pulled up to a fueling station at the dock. He removed a wade of money from a drawer in the bridge cabin. He pulled up to a fueling dock. He had the fuel tank refilled and an additional three gas cannisters to give him fuel to spare. Dr. Sokolov knew that he now had a chance to make it to Jakarta. His main concern now was the weather and turbulence of the ocean. It was going to be a long trip. There were still some risks but running out of fuel would no longer be a likely problem. He believed he would make it now. There he could find a way to revive his research. He paid for the fuel. He screwed the cap back on the fuel tank. He then prepared to sail back out of the port.

CHAPTER 15
BACK TO BASE

Naledi sat on her bunk reading another Agatha Christie novel. This was the fourth book she read in the last two days. Since returning to the ship she did not have much she needed to do. So, she kept to herself and read what was available. Fortunately, the ship had a small library for the crew. As she sat reading the S. S. Hellbender was pulling into the harbor near the base she started from. She turned a page as she heard an announcement come over the ship's PA system. The announcement told her that the ship would be docking within the hour. Naledi was delighted to hear this. She enjoyed reading a good mystery novel, but she was thrilled to be returning to port. Transport helicopters began warming up their engines as the ship pulled into it docking station. A crewman knocked on her cabin door. He eased the door open and said "Miss, you need to get ready to go. Helicopters will very soon fly us back to the base." He told her. Naledi had few personal possessions onboard with her, so she had very little to pack. Naledi was escorted up on the deck to one of two transport helicopters on the deck. She stepped up into the helicopter. She found herself a seat. She sat down and buckled herself in her seat. Once the helicopter was full, it lifted up off the deck and began to fly to the base. Naledi sat still for the short flight to the base. Soon the helicopter landed back onto the base. Naledi unbuckled herself and hurried out of the helicopter. She quickly walked away and back to her room. She looked into the room. She was surprised to see Aldo sitting on the end of her bed. He looked up at her as she walked into the room and stepped toward her bed. She saw his eyes were wet and red. Naledi sat next to him and gave him a hug. Aldo firmly wrapped his arms around her returning her hug. Naledi pushed back against Aldo. She was afraid his embrace was getting too affectionate. She liked Aldo. He was her friend, and she was grateful for all he had done for her. She cared a great deal about him, but she could not allow their relationship to become affectionate. She didn't want to, but she had to push him away. Aldo stepped back away from her. He hung his head low in shame and sadness. Naledi asked him what was troubling him. She handed him paper and a pen, so he could answer her. She closely watched his reply. It was quickly clear to her that he was sad about losing his pervious life and depressed about his future. She tried in vain to comfort and reassure him. As much as she tried, but she could not pull him out of his depression. Naledi thought hard about what she could do to cheer him up. She could but didn't want to hug him again. She didn't want to risk encouraging him affectionately. She could tell him there was a chance to return him to normal. She did not want to possibly give him false hope. She believed it was possible, but very unlikely. She reluctantly told Aldo that there was a very remote chance to reverse the animalistic transformation he had undergone. Aldo smiled and grinned up at her. She was now worried that she had indirectly made a promise to him that she could not keep. How was she going to accomplish what she told him could be done. In big letters he wrote "HOW?" Naledi tried to explain what was needed to be done to have any hope to return him to normal.

CHAPTER 16
JAKARTA

Dr. Sokolov's boat bounced lightly on the ocean surface. He was getting close to Jakarta. He was less than a day away from his destination. He sat back in his chair and read over his experimentation notes on his laptop from his USB thumb drive. He sketched out ideas on how to improve the results. He pulled into a port in Jakarta. His ship was tied to a dock. Dr. Sokolov walked into Jakarta. He heard many languages being spoken as he walked down the streets. He had a long walk out of the port before he reached the streets of the city. He was looking for the Indonesian Institute of Sciences. This was where he hoped he would find access to the equipment he needed. He tried to get directions. He had a hard time to do that because he heard few people speaking English. He heard a serious looking middle age Asian man speaking English. He asked the man for directions. The shorter man with straight black hair asked Dr. Sokolov why he wanted to go to the institute. He tried to explain why he needed access to equipment in the institute without telling him too much. He did tell him he was experimenting DNA and genetic engineering. The man grinned at the doctor. He told the doctor that he knew people might be interested in his experiments. He told Dr. Sokolov to follow him. He wasn't sure he should follow the man, but he had no other choice. Dr. Sokolov followed the man. They got into a taxicab and rode several miles to the other side of the sprawling metropolis. The doctor was surprised to see the cab come to a stop in front of the Embassy of China. He followed this unknown man out of the cab and up the steps to the embassy. The man greeted a well-dressed official. The two men talked together for several minutes as Dr. Sokolov stood in the hallway trying to hear what they were discussing. The two men had a long intense discussion. Occasionally the embassy official looked over curiously at Dr. Sokolov. It made the doctor feel nervous. The discussion between the two men seemed to end in some form of an agreement. They both looked over at the doctor and told him to follow them. He did so, what other choice did he have. They walked down the hall and then turn into a side room. The room appeared to a large elegantly furnished conference room. A large well-polished oak table filled the center of the room. The two men sat in chairs at one end of the table. The embassy official sat at the head of the table. The doctor was told to sit down. He sat in a chair on the opposite side of the table near the two men. "Relax" said the embassy official, "you are safe. We just want to ask you a few questions." Dr. Sokolov was a little nervous. The man that brought the doctor to the embassy official "let me introduce you to Ambassador Cheng Wong. I am Gan Lee an intelligence agent for the Embassy here in Indonesia." He said. "Thank you, Mr. Lee. My name is Dr. Ivan A. Sokolov a doctor of genetics and microbiology." After the introductions were done then Ambassador Wong began to interview and question Dr. Sokolov. He told them his personal information, his educational and career history. The questions then turned to his current work and experiments. A discussion began about his experiments, theories on controlling human evolution and improving the human species.

Ambassador Wong was fascinated by everything Dr. Sokolov had to say about his experiments. The Ambassador looked intently at the doctor. "Dr. Sokolov I know several people that would be very interested in your work. I might even be able to arrange to have you sponsored with everything you need to continue your work," said the Ambassador. The doctor was asked if he had proof of his experimental work. He replied that he had data, notes and photographs of his experiments on a flash drive on a PC aboard his ship. Mr. Lee and Dr. Sokolov rode together in a golf cart across the city back to the port and the doctor's ship. The doctor fetched his flash drive from his laptop on the ship. He slipped the flash drive into his pocket then sat back down in the golf cart. Together he and agent Lee returned to the Chinese embassy. Dr. Sokolov and Mr. Lee returned to the embassy. They walked back into the conference room where Ambassador Wong sat waiting the doctor was guided to a desktop computer. He sat in a chair in front of the PC and plugged in his flash drive. Ambassador Wong flipped a few switches, so the computer screen was also visible on a large 80" plasma TV screen. Dr. Sokolov pulled up the files from his flash drive. He first displayed a series of photos showing the results of his experiments. The men were amazed seeing pictures of a variety of human/animal hybrids. "These animals are the results of your experiments?" asked the ambassador. "Yes, they are!" the doctor replied proudly. "But they look partly human." Continued the ambassador. The doctor answered, "that is because they were in the beginning." "In the beginning? Why would you change a man into an animal? The ambassador was confused. Dr. Sokolov told them that it was not his intention to create full animal transformation. He explained he succeeded in combining human and animal DNA, but he had not yet achieved the level of control he desired. He wanted to give a man the muscles and strength of a bear, but not turn him into a bear. He wanted to give a man the strong eyesight of a tiger not make him a human tiger. He went on to explain that he wanted to control and manipulate DNA so well that he could give humans the best features from many different creatures. "Imagine possibly having the strength of a gorilla and the eyesight of an eagle." He said."That is my goal to build a better human and to personally shape the evolution of man." The doctor grinned with pride as he finished speaking. Ambassador Wong and Mr. Lee went into an intense private discussion, briefly ignoring the doctor. They thanked the doctor for showing them his work. Ambassador Wong reassured Dr. Sokolov that they would get everything he needed to continue his experiments. It was then suggested that they all have dinner. They all had a big and a luxurious dinner together. After the dinner, the doctor was guided to a comfortably plush bedroom. He settled into a plush bed then comfortably slept until morning. They all had a big breakfast the next morning. In the morning Dr. Sokolov was escorted by Ambassador Wong and agent Lee into a limousine. They all drove quickly to the airport. The limousine drove up beside a twin-engine turbo prop airplane with its engines warming up. They all boarded the airplane. The plane rapidly took off shortly after everyone was securely seated. After a couple of hours in the air the plane landed. The doctor asked why they had landed so soon. He was told the plane had landed in Singapore for the sole purpose of topping off the fuel tanks for the long flight ahead of them. After refueling they continued to fly north. Within a few hours they crossed into Chinese air space. The doctor tried to sleep, but the periodic turbulence prevented that.

He ate a meager sandwich about mid-day and drank a South-Asian beer. The plane began to descend. Looking out his window Dr. Sokolov noticed the setting sun. They had been flying almost all day. He asked where they were landing. He was told they were about to land in Jinan, China. A few minutes later the airplane landed then soon came to a stop. Parked next to the plane was a waiting limousine. The doctor was driven to a luxurious hotel suite. He was thrilled to see how plush the suite was. In the suite's bed chamber, he was surprised to see a beautiful black-haired young lady she wore a sheer very low-cut gown displaying her luscious cleavage. The doctor wondered what she was doing there. His hosts told him they wanted to guarantee his comfort and pleasure. He smiled lustfully at the woman. She grinned back at him and invited him to join her. He joined her quickly after stripping down to his boxer shorts. He laid down beside her. As soon as he laid down, she quickly pulled off his boxers and smiled at him. She grinned at him and pulled him close to her. The doctor fell into a blissful sleep after the comfort woman pleasured him to the fullest of her abilities.

CHAPTER 17
AT BASE

Naledi and Aldo sat down at a table together for dinner. Naledi was glad that Aldo had calmed down. She smiled at him as she began eating her dinner. She sipped her drink as she watched her friend carefully. Aldo smiled back. Naledi asked him how he was feeling. He told her that with her help he was feeling better. She then asked him where his home was. She was trying to discover the geographic location of his home and that of his family. She thought it was very important if they were to pursue the slim possibility of returning him to normal. She was also curious to see his home, family, and culture. Naledi had finished her meal and was drinking her second glass of lemonade when her phone rang. She answered the phone she heard a voice she did not recognize. The man on the phone greeted her politely. The man on the phone told her to come to research lab on the base as soon as possible. He told her "We have discovered some interesting things from the DNA of the madman's victims. Your experience might help give us further insight on the new evidence we've uncovered." Naledi, she doubted she would be able to offer any new information. The man insisted that he wanted to meet her and have a conversation with her about the evidence and speculate on the madman's intention. Naledi left the cafeteria and told Aldo she was sorry, but she had to leave. She did not know where she had to go was located. Fortunately, she found someone to guide and escort her to her destination. She stepped inside the laboratory she was instructed to come to. A man in his mid-fifties with well-groomed salt and pepper hair was waiting for her. He wore a lab coat with a calculator and a few luxury pens in his breast pocket. The man greeted her, shook her hand. He introduced himself as Dr. Gerard Randells. Naledi followed Dr. Randells to a desk in the lab. They sat side by side while Dr. Randells displayed a stack of DNA analysis printouts. He gave the printouts for her to study. Naledi was told some of the DNA printouts were from DNA samples of Greg and Frank from before the island mission. Another set of printouts were from current their DNA samples. She studied the two sets of printouts. There was a clear difference between the two sets. She asked Dr. Randell what he thought it all meant. He replied, "The evidence clearly indicates a foreign DNA was injected into their systems and somehow it was made to assimilate into their original DNA and spread throughout their bodies." Naledi asked if he had any idea why it was done. He said "No I do not. Do you have any ideas?" She answered that she had no idea, just her own suspicions, theories or speculations?" They began to converse about the possible purpose of these genetic experiments. Naledi told Dr. Randells that she did not believe it was the madman's goal to transform his test subjects completely from human into animals. "Why do you think that?" asked Dr. Randells. She explained that if the intent were to transform humans into animals the madman would not have needed to keep conducting experiments after the first few times, he transformed people into animals. He must have been trying to achieve something else if he kept conducting experiments. What he was trying to achieve she didn't know, but she was sure it was not complete animal transformations. Naledi and Dr. Randells began discussing the evidence they had. They speculated on the madman's reasoning for conducting these experiments. They speculated wildly on what the madman was trying to achieve.They came to no joint conclusion. They had many theories, but they could not agree on a theory for the madman's motive and goal. Naledi suggested they get more information. She suggested to Dr. Randells how they could get more information. She said they could learn more by discovering what data and information from the madman's laptop. Together they walked over to where the laptop was being analyzed and decoded by computer specialists. They entered the computing lab together. There they met a young man in his early thirties bent over the keyboard console busily entering computer commands. Naledi learned this intense IT geek was David Corner, the top computer specialist on the base. She asked Corner if he had found anything on the laptop. He told her "I have found a lot of files. I am still decrypting a large portion of the data.Dr. Randells asked "Is there anything you can show us yet?" He answered, "there are a few files I could print off for you." Naledi asked "Could you please print off those files? Anything could be helpful." Corner ran a wire from the laptop to a nearby laser printer. Naledi was impatient waiting for the files to be printed. She looked over at Dr. Randells, he was pacing about as they waited. A few minutes later the printer came to life as it began to slowly spit out pages. After the first page came out the printer ran for several more minutes. Dr. Randells pulled out the first several pages and scanned them closely. "This looks interesting." Dr. Randells said as he handed a couple pages to Naledi. She was surprised when she saw the article. The article was entitled "sculpting evolution" She carefully read the article. She first noticed it was written by a Dr. Ivan Sokolov. Now they had a name to go with the experimentation. With a name further investigation could be done. As she read the article began by saying, "For millions of years natural selection has shaped the evolution of life. Now with the discovery of DNA and genetic engineering it is possible for man to shape the future of his own evolution." Naledi exclaimed in shock, "My God, he is trying to redesign humans!" "Damn! It looks like you are right. This guy is insane" replied Dr. Randells. The two of them went into discussion about Dr. Sokolov's goal and motive. As they discussed the situation computer expert Corner said he would have more files decrypted within a few hours and might have all the data decoded by the end of the day tomorrow. Naledi interrupted her conversation with Dr. Randells and said, "I am a bit thirsty and hungry." She exited the room and walked to the cafeteria. Dr. Randells decided to follow her as she left. Naledi went through the serving line. She grabbed a large dish of orange sherbet and a large glass of lemonade. She found a table to sit alone. Dr. Randells sat down with his desert and drink across from Naledi

She began sipping her lemonade and began wondering where the madman Sokolov was.

CHAPTER 18
CHINA

Dr. Sokolov woke up in the soft luxurious bed. He looked over and saw the comfort woman was laying naked next to him. He was smiling broadly. The woman woke up and grinned at him. She pulled him back to her and resumed providing him with her special services of pleasure making. Together they were physically intwined rolling and bouncing firmly around the bed. The ambassador walked in without knocking. First, he praised the woman for the excellent work she was doing. He then addressed Dr. Sokolov and informed him that he would be flown to Peking to meet several high-level government officials. The doctor moaned loud and wildly as the woman brought him to a strong peak of pleasure. The ambassador laughed and exited the room quietly. The pleasure woman kept the doctor in bed the rest of the morning. Near lunch time she led him into the shower and continued caring for him in the shower. The doctor was extremely happy, but physically drained. The woman, the ambassador and the doctor walked to a limousine after lunch. The woman and doctor sat in the backseat. The limo drove to the airport. The limo drove onto the runway and pulled up to a private awaiting Learjet. The ambassador walked up the boarding ladder into the jet. He sat up front. The woman led the doctor up the ladder into the jet. The ambassador looked over at Dr. Sokolov and said "I am glad you are getting along so well with your hostess. Agent Mey Woo is a beautiful and woman and who is very skilled at what she does so well. By your smile I believe you agree with me. Mey will stay with you when we are in Beijing. I will introduce you to all the leaders that want to speak with you when we arrive." The jet took off and left the ground seconds after he finished speaking. The flight was short about an hour before the jet descended and prepared to land. There was a loud screeching sound as the tires of the jet touched the ground. After the jet taxied far down the runway it came to a stop. A huge limousine pulled up and parked beside the jet. The side door of the jet was opened. Mey unfastened the doctor's seat belt. She helped him to his feet. Together they walked down the center aisle and then followed the ambassador out the door and down the stairs into the limousine. The ambassador climbed into the passenger seat in the front of the limo. Mey pulled the doctor into the luxury backseat with her. Mey lustily curled up with the doctor. A minute later the limo drove away. It exited the airport and headed into the center of the city of Beijing. The limo came to a stop in front of a large national bureaucratic building. The ambassador instructed the doctor to exit the limo and follow him into the building. Mey led the doctor by the hand as they followed the Ambassador up the stairs to the building. The doctor felt like a willing dog on a leash as Mey continued to lead him about wherever they went. Despite this uneasy feeling he followed her happily. They walked together into the building. Ambassador Wong led them into a huge conference room. Around a large oak conference table sat four men. One was in a military dress uniform, two in well-tailored suits and one in a lab coat. Ambassador Wong introduced Dr. Sokolov to these men "Let me introduce you to your hosts. First, is General Ju-Long Chang, one of our most highly respected military leaders. Next two major executives in China's national party and government. They are Deshi Chan and Ju Lau. Finally, one of our government's lead scientists, Kun Yang. Gentlemen this is Dr. Ivan Sokolov. He has made some incredible scientific advancements. He is here to present his achievements to us." He told the doctor to make his presentation to everyone. The doctor walked up to the desk. A computer sat on the conference table that was connected to a ceiling mounted LCD projector. He plugged his flash drive into the computer. Dr. Sokolov began by describing his theories of genetic engineering and controlling and shaping the development of human evolution. He described how he successfully mixed human and animal DNA. The men seemed interested in what he was telling them. When he showed them photos of the results of his experiments via the LCD projector, they became much more interested. The men around the table stared at the multiple images of human-animals that the doctor projected up on the large screen. The men spoke excitedly and rapidly amongst themselves. Dr. Sokolov didn't understand Chinese. Even if he did, he would have been lucky to understand more than a few words because they were talking so fast. Mey leaned over and whispered in the doctor's ear "You're a hit, they really like what you have achieved. Your work could be a great benefit to our country." She licked and nibbled at his ear. She turned his face toward her and gave him a big wet kiss. The doctor smiled happily. The Chinese scientist Kun Yang asked, "What do you need to conduct your experiments?" Dr. Sokolov replied by listing all the computing and genetic engineering equipment he would need. He was told any equipment he needed would be made available to him. The doctor told the men in the room he would need test subjects as many as possible. He was told that would be no problem. Ambassador Wong told Mey to take Dr. Sokolov to a deluxe suite in one of the finest hotels in Peking. He also told her to make him as comfortable as possible. Starting now he was her responsibility. Mey began to lead the doctor away from the table. The doctor reached for his flash drive but was told to leave it where it was the men wanted to study everything on it, especially Yang. Mey whisked him out of the room and back into the limousine. They were driven to a supreme luxury hotel. Mey began making him comfortable the second after they entered the Limousine together. Within minutes a finely dressed doorman helped them both out of the limo and into the hotel. The manager behind the front desk greeted them. He was expecting them. He personally escorted them up to their luxury suite on the twenty-fourth floor. The manager smiled at them he told them they were special guests, and all their expenses were paid for by the state. He finished telling them to ask for anything they needed or desired it was all paid for. The manager left. Mey stripped the doctor bare and pulled him naked into the shower with her. He began moaning in pleasure seconds after the warm water sprayed over him. He was going to sleep well tonight.

CHAPTER 19
ON THE RUN

Caleb ran as he tried to put more distance between him and the base, he had been held prisoner in. He was getting hungry he had not eaten since last night before his escape. He knew people would be searching for him soon, so he stayed away from the roads. He was on the run; his freedom was gone. He spotted a rundown small roadside eatery. Maybe there would be a chance for some food. Caleb sat several yards away at the edge of some woods. He watched the movement of people in, out and around the eatery. He was observing what went on in and around the place. As he watched he was planning a course of action to steal some food. He noticed there was almost no one at the rear entrance, except someone brought out the trash and threw it into the dumpster. Caleb crept closer to the rear of the eatery. While the eatery was busy at the front Caleb stealthily snuck in the rear entrance. He was able to sneak into the storeroom unnoticed. He stole a block of cheese and a few pieces of fruit. He also took boxes of milk and a few bottles of juice. After taking what he needed he quickly exited to hide in the woods again. Caleb sat under the cover of the trees and ate and drank. He sat just inside the woods sitting on the line between the wilderness and civilization. As he sat and ate Caleb was thinking of what to do next. The sun was setting Caleb needed to find a place to hide and sleep. It took him some time to find a place to sleep until morning. He finally settled down in a hilly alcove surrounded by shrubs and thick bushes. He finished eating and settled down to sleep. His future was uncertain.

CHAPTER 20
GOING HOME

Naledi laid down in her bunk. She closed her eyes hoping to fall asleep soon. Instead, she laid there thinking to about all that had happened to her recently. It was difficult to sleep with so many unpleasant memories and nightmares about the future racing through her mind. She tossed and turned as her fears swirled around in her head. She finally drifted off to sleep after more than an hour. Her dreams became a kaleidoscope of nightmarish short stories flowing continuously through her mind. She woke up a little bit after dawn. She sat up in her bed but felt exhausted. She was so tired she felt like she had barely slept at all. She stood up. She tried to wake herself up by stretching. As she stretched her phone rang. She could not image who would be calling her now. She answered the phone and recognized the voice of Commodore Mundell. He asked her to join him for breakfast. She agreed than hung up the phone. Naledi slipped her phone in her pocket and began to walk toward the base cafeteria. After she entered the cafeteria, she picked up a tray and chose her breakfast. She took her breakfast tray and looked where to sit. After looking around it was apparent to her that the commodore was sitting alone sipping his coffee waiting for her. She sat down across from the commodore. He looked straight at her and said, "Naledi my dear you have been very helpful in this case." "Thank You Sir!" she replied. He continued "As helpful as you have been, I believe you have contributed as much as you can. You have been asking me when you can go home. I think Now is the time. We will take it from here." Naledi was thrilled to learn she could go home to her apartment. It would be so wonderful to relax at home and try to forget the past few weeks. She smiled happily when she was told a car would be ready to take her home within an hour. Naledi finished her meal and then exited to return to her cabin. She packed her clothes and belongings quickly.

Once her bag was packed, she left the room and walked down the hallway. Exiting the building she saw a large black sedan waiting for her. She sat in the passenger seat. She was about to tell the driver her home address. He told her he knew where to go. The car started and they were on their way. Naledi looked out the window seeing familiar sights as they got closer to her apartment. A few minutes later they pulled up to a stop in front of her apartment. Naledi climbed out of the car and walked up to the front door of her apartment. She pulled her key out of her pocket and unlocked her door. She went inside. She closed the door behind her as if trying to shut out the recent past behind her. She tossed her bag on her bed. She stepped into the bathroom and turned the bathtub faucet on full for hot water. She stripped off her clothes as the tub filled up. She stood naked in the bathroom waiting for the tub to fill up. When the tub was about three-quarters filled up she stepped in the hot water and slowly eased herself down into it. Sighed in pleasure and relief as the hot water wrapped around her and embraced her. She closed her eyes and enjoyed the warmth. She luxuriated in the tub for over an hour. She closed her eyes and enjoyed the heat. As the heat soaked through her body, she could feel tension flow out of her body. The hot bath felt so wonderful Naledi thought she could easily fall asleep in the tub. After all she had been through, she did not want to leave the heavenly feeling of the bathtub. She knew she could not stay in the tub too long, even though she did not want to leave it. A half hour later she stood up and slowly stepped out of the tub. She toweled herself off and walked to her bed. She put on a loose T-shirt and a pair of lavender panties. She laid down on her bed sighing in grateful relaxation. She closed her eyes and tried to empty her mind of all concerns and worries. She was so relaxed she fell deep asleep in minutes. Fortunately, tonight she had no nightmares. Naledi woke up after a long peaceful sleep. She wanted to make herself a nice breakfast, but as long as she had been gone, she could not trust the food in her kitchen. She made and drank a cup of coffee. She ordered an Uber ride to take her into work. She grabbed her purse and waited by her front door. A few minutes later her ride, a blue Taurus, arrived. She sat in the backseat as she headed to work. After the car stopped, she headed up the steps and entered the federal office building. She walked down the hall to the forensics lab, her place of work. It was surprising how everything looked the same as when she was last there. She looked around to see what she could work on now. Her co-workers welcomed her and told her what work needed to be done. She looked at the case and evidence that needed to be analyzed. As she prepared some evidence for DNA processing. There was a knock on the lab door. Naledi looked up and was startled to see Dr. Randells at the door. She felt uneasy seeing him. His presence told her she could not so easily put her adventure behind her. "Damn! It's not over." She thought. "What are you doing here?" asked Naledi. He replied "I need to talk with you. Follow me please." She turned and followed him as they exited and began walking down the hall. Her co-workers saw Naledi leave as quickly as she arrived. They began whispering and gossiping about her as she walked out of sight. He walked down the hall followed by Naledi. She wondered where they were going. Dr. Randells came to a stop just outside the office of her supervisor. "We need to stop here first." Said Dr. Randells. Naledi was curious why they were here. Dr. Randells knocked then he opened the door and entered. He entered and introduced himself. He looked at a short pudgy middle-aged man with short oily black hair sitting behind a large oak desk. "Are you Michael Anders?" asked Dr. Randells. "I am. Who the hell are you?" asked the man behind the desk. Dr. Randells identified himself and then he continued. "have you been contacted by Commodore Mundell?" "I have." Replied Mr. Anders. "Good then you know what is expected to be done." Declared Dr. Randells. Mr. Anders stated, "I understand, but his request must be approved by human resources." It sounded to Dr. Randells as if Anders were trying to deflect the responsibility to someone else. Randells was angry he snapped at Anders "See that it is done. I will hold you responsible. Make it happen if you value your career." Anders snarled back at Dr. Randells he was not used to being treated so harshly. Anders looked angrily at Naledi it was all the young black woman's fault he thought. They exited and continued down the hall. When he found an empty room Dr. Randells pulled Naledi inside. After they both sat down, Naledi looked over at him and asked, "What was that all about?" Dr. Randells looked at her smiled and told her "Naledi, you have been a great help to us on this case. We would not know as much as we do now without you. Also, the Commodore and I both like you. For all the great work you have done for us the commodore insisted you get a promotion and an increase in your pay grade. I agree with him." Naledi blushed. She thanked him very much. He continued "If that putz ever gives you trouble, or a hard time just call me." Naledi asked him what he wanted to talk to her about. She was sure he didn't come just to tell her about a promotion and pay raise. He told her that most of the files on the madman's laptop had been decrypted. He told her that he had read more of the madman Sokolov's files. He now believed her theory of Dr. Sokolov trying to shape and control human evolution was correct. It was clear to him now that the madman Sokolov was trying to create a DIY method for shaping human evolution. Naledi talked with him about this frightening idea. She listened to him as he explained what new information from the decoded files had been discovered. She took in the new information as best she could and thought about it all. Talking with him she knew she was not done with this case as much as she wanted it to go away. She asked him if he understood how the madman transformed people like Greg into animals. Dr. Randells told her he was beginning to understand the process. She asked him how Greg, Frank and Aldo were doing. He told her that Greg and Aldo were getting special counseling. Fortunately, Frank was only showing a few signs of transformation. He warned her of the escape of Caleb. Naledi frowned as she thought about the man that hunted her and tried to kill her. Dr. Randells tried to reassure her by telling her that an agent would be shadowing her and acting as her bodyguard to keep her safe. Naledi thanked him for the information and the protection, but she was still scared. She asked him if they had found Caleb or the mad man Sokolov. He confessed to her that they were still hunting for both. He tried to reassure her that they would catch Caleb. They were sure he could not have gotten too far away from the base. As for Sokolov he was less confident. There was almost any place in the south pacific he could have escaped to. Naledi looked at Dr. Randells she was very serious as she spoke to him "The madman Sokolov has to be found all his files and data destroyed. There is always the chance someone will try to repeat what he has done and was attempting to do. This nightmare must be put to an end it must not continue or be repeated." She stated. Dr. Randells agreed. She thanked him and then left to return to her lab. He bid her a warm farewell and returned to the base.

CHAPTER 21
CALEB RUNNING

Caleb woke amidst the trees. He looked back down at the eatery he raided last night. Out in front of it were parked two sheriff cars. He had to get moving. They might be there just for some breakfast, but Caleb couldn't risk it. He stood up and started jogging through the woods. He needed to steal some wheels. He ran he had to put a lot of distance behind him. As he ran, he looked for opportunities to steal a vehicle. Fortunately, he saw over the highway signs for the Airport. He began moving in that direction. It took him well into the afternoon, but he finally made it to the airport. He slowly approached the airport from the open field between the runways. As he got closer to the airport building, he looked at the markings on the aircraft. He was pleased to see a few cargo planes that belonged to commercial mail carriers. He stealthily moved toward the cargo planes. He thought his best chance was to sneak on and stowaway on a cargo plane. He moved up as close as he dared, while still staying under cover. He smiled as he saw a FedEx plane being loaded. He watched as many boxes and packages were loaded into the plane. It did not take long for three workers to load the plane. After the last packages were loaded the workers drove off. Caleb saw them drive away. He knew this was his chance. He ran from his hiding spot to the open cargo door. As Caleb got close the door was slowly starting to close. He leapt up inside the door as it was rising up and was closing. He was inside. He would leave Hawaii far behind. Caleb crawled over the boxes as the door closed. He sat between boxes and sat down. As he sat, he could feel the plane liftoff. He did not know where the airplane was going, but it didn't matter. He was leaving his enemies behind. He would not be living in prison. He looked at the hundreds of packages around him. While looking around he saw boxes from Land's End. He ripped open the packages. He found a lot of blankets and winter wear. He put on a winter jacket, gloves, and scarf. He put on all the winter wear he could find to protect himself from sub-zero temperatures when the plane cruised at a high altitude. He sat down again and covered himself with blankets. He was safe and on his way.

CHAPTER 22
EPILOGUES

Naledi returned to her lab and continued the work she had begun. She tried to ignore her co-workers as they glared at her and talked about her. She felt uncomfortable being in the midst of jealous and suspicious people. The phone rang on the desk. One of the lab technicians answered the telephone. The technician hung up the phone. He turned to Naledi and said, "Mr. Anders wants to see you Now." "Why?" Naledi asked. "I don't know." Replied the technician. Naledi left the lab again. Everyone was chattering about her as she walked out. She walked into Mr. Anders office. She could see he looked angry. Mr. Anders glared at her and shouted at her "Who the hell was that with you this morning? How dare you bring someone here to talk so abusively to me." Naledi tried to explain who Dr. Randells was and that it was not her idea to visit his office this morning. Mr. Anders said he would give her the promotion and raise he was told to give her. He told her that was all he would do for her and that he would keep a critical eye on her. Naledi acknowledged his message behave right or else. She bid Mr. Anders good day and walked back to the lab. Everyone was staring at her as she re-entered the lab. Naledi was glad it was almost lunchtime. She went out alone to her favorite local restaurant. After lunch she finished the day working on her own in the lab. She avoided everyone else as much as they avoided her. At the end of the workday. She ordered an Uber to return home to her apartment. She tried to forget the day as she relaxed in a hot bath.

Dr. Sokolov woke up in the luxury bed. He smiled as he woke up because Mey was giving him plenty of thrilling attention. Mey called for a good room service breakfast for them both. Mey pulled him out of bed and then lead him into the shower. She washed him thoroughly in the shower. After drying off they sat down the breakfast that was delivered to their suite. Dr. Sokolov while staring at sexually gorgeous Mey as she quickly dressed in a comfortable and very revealing outfit. She grabbed the doctor by the hand and led him outside and down the hallway. She pressed herself against him as they rode the elevator down. Mey pulled him out of the elevator, across the lobby into a limousine waiting for them just outside the main entrance. They sat together in the backseat. Mey curled up tight against the doctor. She nibbled his earlobe, kissed his neck, and massaged his groin. She said in his ear that today he needed to work well today. The limo drove to a secret location. Mey led Dr. Sokolov through several security checkpoints. She opened doors with a special i.d. card. She led him into the secret room and showed him around his laboratory. She told him to work hard. She told him if he worked hard, she would work hard on him when he returned to the suite tonight. She kissed him passionately, then left him to do his work. He looked over all the equipment and supplies. They had provided him with everything and more. He began preparing for his next experiment. He had so much to work with, but then he realized he did not have a test subject. He told this to one of the two assistants he was provided. The assistant left the lab for a few minutes. He returned pushing a gurney with a young woman strapped tightly down to the gurney. The woman's eyes were wide open with an expression of great fear on her face. The doctor withdrew a vial of blood from her. The blood was placed in a DNA analyzer. He waited for the analysis to be completed. Dr. Sokolov sat with his assistants. He talked with them and learned about them and how qualified they were to assist him in his work. He continued preparing his test subject and analyzing her DNA. This would be interesting he never had a female test subject before. It would create several new opportunities and difficulties as well. The day went by quickly. Mey returned at five o'clock to pick the doctor up. Together they rode in the limo back to the suite. Mey kissed and questioned him about his day. He told her everything. He asked her advice about having a female test subject. After they ate a fancy dinner in the suite, Mey tended to Dr. Sokolov with her special talents. A few hours later he was drained of energy and sexually satisfied before he fell quickly and deeply asleep.

CPSIA information can be obtained
at www.ICGtesting.com
Printed in the USA
BVHW050027260422
634897BV00004B/13